Finch Books by Author

Single Books
The Cinder City Embers: Singularity

A Cursed Crow
The Seven Year Crow
The Court of Less

A Cursed Crow

THE COURT OF LESS

LANNE GARRETT

The Court of Less
ISBN # 978-1-80250-542-9

Interior text design by Claire Siemaszkiewicz
Finch Books

Published in 2023 by Finch Books, United Kingdom.

Finch Books is an imprint of Totally Entwined Group Limited.

THE COURT OF LESS

Dedication

Hi, Mom and Dad!

Come away, O human child!
To the waters and the wild
With a faery, hand in hand,
For the world's more full of weeping than you can understand.

—excerpt from *The Stolen Child* by W. B. Yeats

Elphame
~ Alfheim ~
The Golden Court
Spring Court
Seelie Courts
Summer Court
The Court
of Blood
and Bones
Wildelands
The Gate
The Court of
Shadows
The Court of Less
Unseelie Courts
The
Hallows
~ Tylwyth ~
Winter Court
Autumn
Court

Chapter One

"Foolish little Crow, you've unleashed the darkness onto these Golden Lands."

Solas' words echoed into the night and pushed me from the dead king and burning kingdom of those who had caged me. Behind us, the Golden Court trembled under the cruel touch of a long-caged hell released from its belly. They would be the last court to Take me—a promise I made to myself when I'd struck the match on my way out of the dungeons that had once held me. Setting it to burn had lit a fire within my soul.

A certainty fell over me as I ran. I wasn't afraid to die for freedom or what it would take to keep it. My fear rested in living, of being forced inside another prison and never tasting a choice that was my own. If Elphame had taught me anything, it was that nothing was free—not for Fae and not for a Crow on the run with a gnome and a fairy. And as we ran from Alfheim, I knew I'd pay for what I had done.

The Golden Forest plunged us into ominous darkness. The moon above and the carnage we left behind roused creatures, and the curious, rapacious beasts crawled out of their lairs, awoken by the smell of blood in the air, the promise of flesh and their duty to protect their cursed court. I muffled my screams, caught them in my throat and saved them for later, but I still jumped and twitched with each new squall and bloodcurdling cry that echoed through the forest and crawled up my spine. I watched as the trees came alive, transforming into a lethal playground. Whenever something bravely approached us, readying for a feast of traitors, they would be taken by something scarier, snatched off the ground and torn up through the treetops and into the sky above.

The lands around Alfheim, where no one freely ventured, were the deadliest. It was their first defense against invaders, and we willingly ran through them, through the monsters too fearsome and hideous to invite out of the shadows. I could feel them slowly pressing in around us, but I didn't stop running. I couldn't. The choices were to be eaten on the run or be caught and dragged back. I'd sooner become the next meal of a creature than ever step foot back into the Golden Manor. I could think of a dozen worse ways to die within the Golden Court, none of them as merciful as ending in the belly of a beast.

Tree branches grabbed at me, igniting my fear of being found. The limbs stretched out in front of me, blinding me to my way. The forest closed around us, forming a cavern of distorted arms and legs that reached for me as I passed. As I stumbled and staggered, tripped and skinned layers from my pants and soon, my bare knees, I didn't stop running. Running was the only power I had that was my own, the only thing that would grant me the remotest of chances. I turned the pain and fear and the months of becoming one of them—one of the hideous beasts of the courts—into fuel. I left that person behind—the monster—and ran from her as much as I ran from the court that helped create her.

Pain clamped my chest like a deadly vise, and my lungs begged me to slow. My legs felt like rubber after miles of jogging at a constant pace. I swallowed down selfish breaths of air, never getting enough. But not even my starving lungs caused me to stop. Each time I fell, Nix was there, pushing and pulling until I got back up. The fear on his face drove me to stand each time. My feet dragged noisily on the carpet of moss and leaves and kicked up an easily trackable route. I hadn't been worried about hiding my footprints, for it wasn't mere mortals who would be hunting us.

"Close, Perdi—almost at the border," Nix whispered from my side.

"Thank God," I groaned. Despite my weak state, I curled my mouth into a smile. We approached the border, and the realization that I had actually escaped the Golden Court finally struck me.

We were stopped twice before we were free of the Golden Court. Both times, those who had found us let us go, for no other reason than what we had done for two dozen prisoners. The creature I had freed from the muck had spread the word of what we had accomplished. We had risked our lives to save those who were weaker, and for that, they would say they hadn't see us. I took the freedom but left the gratitude behind. I didn't want to be a hero, but I didn't want to be a prisoner, either.

We climbed over a rock wall and landed on the other side—the Summer Court. The pace slowed, but the danger was not over and wouldn't be for several days. Yet, I still felt smug about my small win. I was free from the clutches of King Aelfdene and his court of subjects, those who were mirrors of their leader. Once we crossed out of Golden Territory, I breathed a little deeper. The stench of flowers was almost gone, along with the tightness in my chest. I hadn't realized how putrid the air had been until I took my first deep breath of something other than funerals.

The heat never changed as we crossed the border from the Golden Court—the capital of the Seelie Courts—into the Summer Court. The only difference was the cool breeze, and the stench of floral arrangements had almost disappeared. The grass was green but sunbaked in areas. The trees blossomed in brilliance but lacked the magick of the Golden Court. Where King Aelfdene forced perfection, the Summer Court allowed its natural flaws, and that's what made it beautiful. The broken flowers, too heavy to hold their heads high, its mud and rocks and ugly barked trees had made it feel more like home than the Golden Court ever could. The reality of my freedom sank in as I pressed my hands into the rough tree. I was free. Even if it didn't last, it was still worth it.

"We need shelter," I said through my gritted teeth. My legs began to shake and cramp. I was tired, scared, cold and hungry. "I'm not feeling too good here."

"We need to keep going. We can't stop, not yet," Nix called back. "We need to get away from the estate of the Summer King, Morrow. To save his court, he'll send us back."

I cursed under my breath. "I'm not Fae. I can't keep going." My body tingled. I had used up all my magick and energy to get as far as I had, and there was nothing left in me to give.

"Just a little farther… We can stay in one of the fox dens up ahead." He compromised once he saw me crawling through the dirt on my hands and knees.

I slinked on all fours, too tired to stand. I bargained with the gods and goddesses for just a bit more energy to make it to shelter. They hadn't ever heard my prayers before, but today they might just think it was funny enough to let me live. Nix walked at my side and griped that he wasn't big enough to carry me. He said he was strong enough, but my weight wouldn't be balanced and I'd collapse around him, pinning him beneath me. The thought made me laugh.

"We're here," he announced and pointed to a dark hole in the ground at the base of a tree. "You rest, and I'll find food."

He didn't need to convince me to climb in. I maneuvered my body into the mouth of the den and scooted in feet first in case something was in there that needed a kick. Inside the dirt mound was a twenty-by-twenty room carved out of the earth by claws too big to think about. It was large enough for me to stand, jump up and not touch the ceiling.

"You probably don't want to see what an Elphame fox looks like," he said, to my surprise.

"What are the chances that it'll come home tonight?" I asked.

He shrugged. "I wish I could say zero, but the odds are extremely low. Mating season is here. They move up the mountain to find a mate. They'll remain there until they need to give birth. Then, they'll come home. We won't want to be anywhere near here when they're ready to birth."

"And what exactly do I do if it comes back and you're not here?"

He laughed. "It won't matter if I'm here or not. We'll all three be dead, one after the other."

"I don't know why I expected anything less than death," I replied.

Nix went to forage, and my creature hovered at the entrance, keeping guard. The shadows in the crevices eased my weary bones, and when they moved, I relaxed. I picked a spot on the straw in the corner and closed my eyes. The ground was cold, as was my body. I shivered until the familiar warmth of darkness settled over me, and for once since coming to Elphame, I thought I had a good chance of surviving. I wasn't scared. I was free. It didn't matter to me how long I remained free, as long as I died that way. With a sigh that vibrated against the dark, I slept deeply, sleeping to the hum of dozens of soft voices.

For three hours, not even the gods, who ignored me at a constant, could have woken me from my slumber. Not even Nix or my creature could get through the shadows to wake me. Each time they tried, they hit a solid mass of black. When I woke and crawled from inside my cocoon, the shadows were gone as quickly as they had come. Nix was pacing and had marched a dent into the earth in front of my makeshift bed.

"Do you know what that is?" Nix yelled at me. My creature sat on his shoulder, shrilling words I couldn't understand.

"The dark?" I asked.

"Yes, the dark. The mist. The bloody brick wall of shadows that I couldn't get through. Do you know what that is?" he asked again.

"No, not really," I answered. "They came to me when I first got to the Golden Court, then again when I was being lashed. They've been coming around since my first day. They helped me bring down the stone wall in the basement of the Golden Court."

"They are what our nightmares are about. We don't need any more nightmares, Perdi."

I knelt beside his mound of food and ate. I was starving. I stuffed my mouth full of berries and roots, leaves and fruits. Nix had refilled our canteens with fresh spring water, and it tasted like liquid gold. After filling my stomach, I leaned against the wall and smiled. I had eaten some of the best meals that all Elphame could provide, but this was the finest I had eaten in all my life.

"I couldn't get to you. Neither of us could. I couldn't smell you anymore. I couldn't feel you." He sat on my knee and hung his head. "It scared me. I didn't know what to do."

"I'm sorry. I didn't know. Solas was able to get to me before," I answered.

"Solas can reach into hell and pluck the wings off a demon," Nix replied. "You need to stop calling to them."

"I'm not calling them. They just come."

"You *are* calling them. You just don't realize it. The darkness has only answered to one, and you don't want him coming on the fires of hell next time. Perdi, he is feared by all, and we released him. He eats the souls of all. Do *not* call on his shadows, lest you wish him to follow them back to you."

"Who?" I asked. "Solas?"

Nix shook his head. His eyes darted from corner to corner. "No. Not even I will say his name in the dark. He is made of shadows and stolen souls, and you just busted him out of his prison. Just stop, okay?"

"What's the plan for today?" I asked, and he let me change the subject.

"Same as yesterday. More running, hiding, fear, the usual." Nix jumped off my knee and began to pack up our gear. "Perdi, we have to get to the Court of Less."

"I saw Solas in the hall before I killed the king. He told me to go to the Courtless Lands. That it was the only place where I won't be hunted."

"It's the only place the other kings will not venture and live," he replied.

"Besides Solas," I countered. "Something tells me he goes wherever the hell he wants."

"Well, there's that." Nix laughed.

"I freed his people, didn't I? Doesn't that buy us something? Won't they help me?" I asked.

He shook his head. "Don't count on it. And for the record, of those locked in the dungeon, not all of them belonged to Solas. What you freed—what terrifies us all—answers to no one, and you let it go without asking a favor in return, a payment for their freedom. He gave us a head start, as promised. Now he doesn't owe you anything."

"Great, let's add them to the list of people to run away from."

"Perdi, there is no list. We simply run from everyone, regardless of who they are. No lies or pretending, it doesn't matter who it is. We run from them until we get to the Court of Less."

"Remember all those survival classes they made us take growing up? Years of training on how to protect ourselves if ever we were Taken, and I can't wait to tell them it's a gigantic waste of time," I half joked. "Nothing I've learned has come in handy. Why would I build a fire and signal to all Elphame where I am?"

"It is to keep you warm so you don't freeze to death. The fire isn't what will show Fae where you are, Perdi. They can smell you long before they'd see the smoke."

"That's not very comforting," I muttered.

"It wasn't meant to be," he replied. "Least comforting of all is they will know where we're headed. It's where everyone goes who is on the run. Courtless Lands are the only safe haven. Fire, no fire, smell or not, they'll know that is where we're going. If they were smart, they'd just wait for us at the border."

We finished our lunch, and my little creature lifted a small leaf of paste for the cuts on my hands. Once it touched my wounds, the burning stopped and brought a sigh of relief. She fluttered in and out of the den, bringing back plants and seeds, which I wrapped up and stuffed into my bag for her.

"I'm sorry, Nix," I whispered.

"It's okay. Just leave the dark alone," he answered.

"No, I mean, for everything. I'm sorry I brought you back here and for subjecting you to that awful place." My eyes watered and my nose tingled. My tears were close to falling. "I didn't think of how all this would affect you or hurt you. I'm so sorry you're in this mess. I'm sorry you had to watch all of that happen and be powerless to stop it."

He climbed onto my crossed legs. "You didn't drag me here. I choose to come. You didn't subject me to anything. *They* did. Do not take responsibility for them, don't ever do that."

I nodded and wiped away the few tears that had escaped. "I know it may sound bad, but I'm thankful you're with me."

"Me, too. But the next time you plan to kill a king, let me know first. I'll be a little more prepared." He laughed. "I was in my sleeping gown, for God's sake. What possessed you to kill him, anyway? That was a pretty provocative move, even for you. We spent months building your lies, and in a hot minute, you made your final move."

"I bet no one saw that coming," I joked.

"Not even I did."

"Every single night, I could hear them scream. After the banquets, the parties, the dinners, Aelfdene would pick one woman, sometimes barely of age, and would force her into his bedchamber. He'd drag them down the halls by their hair. I'd hear them begging for help, followed by him laughing. They were just meat to him." I cringed at the memories of their cries, their pain and my own inaction. "I was always too scared to help. I was terrified he would pick me to replace them. I didn't want to take their place in his bed. I just wanted it to stop. I wanted *him* to stop. I needed to know he'd never do it again. The only way I could guarantee he'd stop was to kill him."

"Do you regret it?" he asked.

"No. Not even if I die because of it," I answered. "I'd do it again, only slower."

"He needed to die, Perdi." Nix patted my hand. My creature nodded.

"Yes, he did. Elphame is a better place without him."

"Let's hope the son who takes his throne doesn't revel in the same delights. I'd hate to have to return for you to kill him, too. It's a long journey back." He grinned. "It's time to go."

I pulled on my pack and started to climb from the den into the light. I much preferred the darkness, where I could hide. I followed him out of our false safety and back into the hunt for a Crow.

This time, we were walking and not running. I was thankful for the slower pace. My body needed the break. My wounds required time to scab. We stayed undercover and stopped when we heard the faintest of noises. Nix ran up ahead every so often and returned to tell us it was a bird or an animal or something to avoid. My creature zipped in and out of the trees, her wings as fast as a hummingbird's. At times, Nix would make us go back and find a different route, either because he had run across a farm with Fae in the field or because the animal was big enough to eat us. Other times, he would march us past a farm and farmers with bushels of food, a thank you for what we did. Nix had said the news had spread across all Elphame and likely into the mortal realm. A Crow had escaped with all the prisoners and killed a king who was feared by all on her way out.

"A Crow, a gnome, a creature and a slave escaped the Golden Court and freed everyone along the way." He was proud of himself. "I couldn't make this stuff up if I tried. If it weren't an immediate death sentence, I'd be shouting it from the rooftops."

"I certainly hope everyone is as happy about this as you are," I answered back and threw my apple core into the bushes. I stopped in my tracks. My apple hit something with a thud and a scurry. "Nix, we're being followed."

"Like I wouldn't notice? Nothing escapes the nose of a gnome. Give me some credit here. They're with her." He pointed his thumb to my creature. He jumped down from my shoulder and whistled. From every branch and fallen tree, small creatures came out from their hiding spots. "They travel in packs. They've never been too far away. But in the Golden Court, they'd have been killed, so they waited in the trees."

"They're so cute—terrifying, but cute." I laughed as I was swarmed. The joy I found in my laughter surprised me. It felt like a lifetime had passed since I laughed with the full force of my soul.

"You can't keep them, Perdi," he teased. "One is bad enough, and she's a pain."

For the next three hours of walking, the creatures didn't hide, but mine was the only one who rode on my shoulder. Her shrills, from her perch, sent the group up and down, left and right. She commanded them, tucked into my hair, warm from my body. When one strayed, she would grab them, scold them and come back to me. She was scary when she wanted to be, and not many of her people tested her patience. I likely wouldn't, either.

Nix told me stories of the Summer Court, ruled by King Morrow. He was as cruel as the next but wasn't feared for his dungeons or his taking of the unwilling. He was known for being vicious in war and protective of his people and family. The smallest slight was war, plain and simple. I could respect his ruthlessness. If he wasn't willing to do what it took to keep his people or family safe, no one else here would. His territory spread along the entire bottom of the Seelie Court, and there was no way around it. It edged the river that was used to bring me to the Golden Court on the barge of the dead. It was the river that separated the Seelie Court from the Unseelie, with the Courtless Land spanning the top.

"How do we get over the water?" I asked. "I'm not getting in it. I know that much."

"I'm not getting in the water, either. What a waste of a trip this would be, only to be eaten," he answered. "That's not even our biggest problem. We have to get *to* the water first. The grounds won't be as deserted as they were on your arrival."

"Naturally," I grumbled under my breath.

"Perdi, we've come this far. We can do this. When we get to the water—and we will—there are a few bridges, and if the barge is there, I can bargain for transportation."

"I wish I had your confidence." I smiled weakly.

"If we were in the Court of Blood and Bones or the Court of Shadows, I would be more concerned about trying to sneak around. But once you've been to those two courts, this isn't nearly as scary. The first one, no one has ever made it back out of. The second, without an invite, is a quick death, no questions."

As the night sucked the sun from the sky, we took refuge in an old cabin no bigger than my old bedroom in Whitwick, that looked much like the abandoned cabins in the hills back home. I tried to ward the doors and windows, but each time I did, the creatures and Nix would be dragged outside by a wind of my making. There were too many cracks and crevices for my spell to work and not bounce wildly around, seeking something to grip. Nix tried to tell me to keep the wards and they'd sleep outside, but I couldn't risk them. If my friends died because of me—by weather, creature or Fae, when I could have given them a better chance at surviving—I'd hate myself. I wouldn't separate us. We were stronger together, no matter how big any of us were or weren't. In Elphame, size was not a deciding factor.

Together, we hunkered down in the farthest corner, under old and musty blankets that smelled of years of weather and animals. Together, I felt tougher, like we could take on whatever came through the door or walls. I tucked Nix and my creature into my jacket for warmth and willed my bones and muscles to relax. As hard as I tried, my muscles remained flexed, ready to bolt from danger.

"I feel strange here…like every nerve is alive." I twisted around. I felt antsy and restless.

"It's Elphame. You're feeling the constant thrum of energy and magick. The longer you're here, the more like here you'll become."

"I don't want to become Fae."

"Elphame doesn't really care much for what you want, Perdi. It's what happens to mortals of Fae blood who come here."

Another reason to hate the place was added to my list, which had grown into a book.

"Do you think we'll make it?" I asked, fearing the answer. "No lies."

"I hope so," he finally answered as if he'd weighed our options first. "If we don't, we died free, and there's no better death than a free one."

"Solas will find me. I can feel it. I can hear them, his people. I can hear the flap of their wings, their groans rolling across the clouds. They're not far from here." I said what we all knew and didn't want to acknowledge. "I can smell him on the wind from their wings."

"As do I. Together, they are the very darkness that haunts Elphame."

"How do I kill the darkness?" I whispered in fear that they'd hear me.

"You can't. You just hide."

"If Solas controls the Sluagh, why didn't I see any of them at court, protecting him?"

"They're always a few steps behind him and would have rained down like fire from the sun had Solas needed help. But he doesn't need help or protection. He's a force on his own."

I nodded. "If I'm caught, will they kill me for what I did to the king?"

He popped his head out of my sweater and hugged me as best he could. "Yes. No. I don't know. They'll either want your head or sentence you to prison. You killed their king, Perdi. How else should they respond? To do nothing would show weakness. As you've learned, weakness is not an affordable commodity in Elphame. But honestly, no Crow has ever had the gumption to attack a Royal, let alone kill one. Though I'm sure they'll be adding that to the next negotiations."

"I'm not that brave. I was terrified to my core."

He kissed my nose. "Yes, you are. Bravery doesn't mean you're not scared. It means you still rise to the occasion. And as it turns out, sometimes that occasion is killing a king."

"You've read too many mortal books, Nix," I replied, my small laugh quieting into a yawn. "I killed someone. I've never killed someone with my bare hands."

"You should rest, Perdi. Don't think about things you can't change or things you don't want to change." He slunk back down into my sweater. "Tomorrow comes fast when you're exhausted."

I nodded but had one more question. "What about the oath? Will they kill me for leaving? Will the mortal world suffer for what I've done?"

"You didn't break any oaths since you're technically still in Elphame. The oath says you must remain here, as the Crow, for seven years, but it doesn't say where in Elphame you must remain. It's an agreement among the Fae where the Crow will live, not part of the oath with mortals. Teind, the tithe we pay to the Gods, is for a sacrifice to Elphame. You're still here, so I don't see how they could call you an oath breaker and ask for your life as payment. We're walking a fine line, but you haven't crossed it."

I had no more questions. He had no more answers.

I wondered if we'd make it through the night.

We scheduled turns to keep watch. We ate a snack, and I gave my creature a drop of my blood since she couldn't eat what we had. I offered her a leaf with several drops of my blood for her people as a thank you. She seemed surprised by the offer but eventually took it. The others, scattered around the room, each took a taste. With my blood on their lips, the creatures blanketed us while we slept. They kept watch in appreciation for my life essence.

I slept, finally, once my body realized it wouldn't be able to fight without rest. I dreamed of darkness, the cabin and its inability to protect us, with walls as broken as I. The howling from the forest had slinked into my dream and haunted me, followed me. Creatures I couldn't see nipped at my ankles. I dreamed of eating them, of letting my Malice out like twisted black roots and letting her feast on the souls of others. Rather than winding my Malice around their souls and forcing them to feel what I wanted them to feel, I pulled. I yanked with all my might and took away everything that kept their hearts beating—their very will to live—as I drank them down, refilling my cup of magick with their energy. The darkness from the dungeon watched from the shadows I had created with the souls I had taken.

"Why are you here?" I glanced to my right to see a man standing in swirling shadows.

"Because you are here. Save your energy. You cannot eat them all."

His mouth didn't move, but I heard every word as if he were whispering into my ear.

"I'm not here. I'm dreaming. I can feel it. I feel Nix curled into my neck as though he were here right now. I can hear my creature."

"Think, little Crow. Why do you hear your creature? What could make her shrill so loudly?"

I thought about it for a moment. *Trouble*. I only hear that noise when there is trouble.

"You need to wake up. The real games are about to begin."

"I don't want to play anymore."

"If you don't open your eyes now, when you do, you will play games you do not wish to play."

"Don't leave me."

Chapter Two

My creature's shrill brought me from a restless sleep inundated with images and sounds of death, souls eaten, lives taken and the darkness from the dungeon. Her penetrating scream bled into the dream and became part of the nightmare until my entire body twitched in panic. But it was too late. The warning had come long after I could do anything about it. I didn't try to run. There would be no use. There'd be nowhere to go, no safety for me to get to. To my utter surprise, it wasn't Solas who found us first. It was Faolan. I didn't know which was worse, my enemy or my enemy's enemy?

"Good morning, Perdi." Faolan crouched down and smiled. His smile pulled an ugly look from my face. He once had the softest of expressions, a kind of warmth that pulled me in. Now it was cold and calculating. "You've made it farther than I thought you would. I'm impressed. These aren't lands easily crossed."

I cursed under my breath as I stared into his ice-blue eyes. The eyes I had loved, which once drowned me, now pierced the broken parts of my heart like a knife. Bottomless pools of selfishness rippled beneath his carefully masked face. But he'd never be able to hide his truth from me again. It had been lashed into my body. I carried the scars of his lies on my back.

Fear crushed me like a pillow on my face. I sat up and scrambled backward until my back hit the dilapidated wall. The movements shot pain through my tired and aching muscles. The memory of him coming into my cell in the Golden Court brought tears to my eyes. Each breath was a struggle against the tightening in my chest. My head whirled, and I forced myself to calm, to breathe, to be present. Staring at the man who had sold me to the devil was the push I needed. The anger pulled my head above water, and I homed in on the moment.

"What do you want?" I finally squeaked out. My voice was not nearly as calm as I wanted it to be. But it didn't matter how steady a voice I had. I was scared when I killed the last king. I'd be just as scared if I were forced to do it again.

"As I said before, you. *You.*" Faolan stood and offered his hand. I didn't take it. "Surely even you can see the predicament you are in. You will die out here, Perdi. The vultures are circling as we speak. Come… I give my word. No harm will come to you on my lands."

I raised my eyebrows. Did he actually expect me to go with him willingly, as though I trusted him as I once had? The look on his face—the pride, the surety—told me he thought more highly of himself than I did.

"Trust no one." My answer was firm.

"Speaking of your little dog, as you called him for all the court to hear, what has he said to have you hate me in such ways?"

"Nothing," I answered, and that was the truth. "It is you who caused this hate, Faolan. You are a liar and a traitor. You sold me out the first chance you got. You used me. You did it when I needed you most, and I'm sure you'll do it again."

"Sadly, Perdi, it was not I who sold you out. It was your own people who did that. I did what I could once your neck was on the chopping block."

"Not even you believe the lies you're telling. I have heard of what the Guardian has done, but you, Faolan? You marked me as a child then came for collection," I answered. "I don't need your excuses, so don't bother with them."

"I was not the one to curse you to Elphame. Whether you believe that or not, we don't have time for this right now. I've tried to be kind. I've tried to explain. But now you're leaving me no choice." He grabbed me with incredible speed and force, knocking the air from my chest. Faolan was both High Fae and of Royal Blood. My Malice did nothing more than place a knowing grin on his face. "*Tsk, tsk,* Perdi. Some magicks are better left in the dark, where they belong."

"One day, I'll be strong enough, and my Malice will eat your tarnished soul," I countered through gritted teeth.

"But today is not that day."

He bear-hugged me, lifted me off the ground and dragged me from the one-room cabin into the brilliant daylight. My eyes burned from the sudden brightness, spotting my vision with shadows. I scanned the trees, blinking past the blotches. His men surrounded the cabin, but not a creature was in sight. I half wished they were still there, attacking. But sacrificing them for the off chance that I'd get a few feet between Faolan and me just wasn't worth it.

"Please, Faolan, let me go." I stopped struggling and turned my body to face him. "If you ever cared for me at all, you'd let me go."

"Are you seriously going to try to bargain with me now? You don't even know what you're negotiating for. You should have more sense than that, in a land of Fae who will twist oaths that will bind your children's children." Faolan shook his head. "It's time to move."

"Run, Nix!" I yelled and twisted from Faolan, landing on my back.

"Not so fast, little man," Faolan grabbed Nix before he could climb out of my jacket and held him by his waist. Nix didn't cry out or fight or ask me for help. That pained me more that he was used to being abused, to the point that he didn't cry and didn't show fear.

"Run," Nix called out, but I froze, staring at him in the grips of Faolan. Nix wouldn't have left me under any circumstance. He came into hell with me. I couldn't leave him.

"What will it be, Perdi? Are you going to get up and walk willingly, or do I need to knock you both out?" Faolan proposed two impossible choices. "I'd prefer you to walk willingly, but unconscious would be quicker."

"Perdi, let me die," Nix said calmly, and it broke me.

"There's no point in your death when he's going to drag me there, anyway," I answered. "Give him to me, and I'll come."

"Deal." Faolan tossed Nix, and I caught him. The storm inside my stomach calmed the moment I had Nix back. I carried Nix in my jacket, away from Faolan and his people.

Faolan put his arm under mine and around my back. "Hold on, Perdi. Should you wish me to not drop you."

"Why?" I asked and gripped him as we moved through the trees, my feet not touching the ground. In flashes, I caught bits and pieces of the view—the mountain ranges and landmarks I had memorized. I knew where we were going and the route we were taking. There was no point in running. There would be nowhere to hide. As we approached the river, Faolan pulled me tighter into his body, and in a blast of icy wind, we were over the water and on the other side, with not a drop on our feet. He didn't slow. Faolan pulled us across the lands with speeds that forced me to tuck my face into his shoulder. When he let me go, I staggered and vomited.

"That felt awful," I groaned. I felt scattered. The sudden change in weather chattered my teeth. Unseelie lands were the opposite of Seelie. Where there had once been heat and sun and flowers surrounding us, there was now cold, moss and the smell of Christmas. "What the hell was that? I didn't know Fae could fly."

"Unless we have wings, we can't," Nix explained. "It's an exaggeration of speed. Some of us can just do it better. You get used to it."

"I don't ever want to do that again," I grumbled.

"We made it over the water," he whispered.

I stood and looked around, my senses finally catching up with me. "Where are we?"

"Unseelie Territory, the Winter Court," Faolan answered from behind me. His court. There would be no friends here, and I didn't count on finding one anywhere in Elphame.

"What are you going to do to me?" I asked Faolan.

"Nothing more than I promised you," he replied.

"I'm going to need more than that if you want me to willingly go to your court. You're demanding I give up my freedom. Why? For what?"

"We'll save our secrets for our wedding night, shall we?"

"Wedding?" I blurted. "I'm not going to marry you, Faolan."

"You're a Crow, Perdi. You have no say here. By rights, I now own you."

"It's not happening, Faolan. I'm *not* marrying you," I repeated and backed away from him.

"Don't you remember, Perdi, you agreed to marry me years ago?" His grin was as sly as he was.

"I was a child, Faolan."

"Good enough for me. Good enough for Elphame. Once we are oathed, no one will have the power to take you from my lands. Nothing and no one can force me to release you to them."

I looked down at Nix. My eyes watered and my pulse hammered. I wouldn't face the same fate as every other woman forced into the bed of a king. I shook my head over and over. I wasn't just another prisoner. I would be another victim. I wouldn't survive it. I would rather die a thousand horrible deaths than spend one night under Faolan.

"No, no, no," I whispered as I walked. I stared at Nix, pleading with him for a plan. I could see my fate playing out before my eyes. On the other side of a massive forest, I'd never get free. Another hour and I'd be trapped into a life I promised myself I'd never walk willingly into. I wouldn't be caged again.

"Run," Nix whispered and looked to my left. "We're so close. *Run.*"

I tucked Nix in tightly against my body and bolted to the trees. My feet sank into bone-deep cold puddles. Bits of slush made me grip for balance. My boots, made for the Summer Court, did nothing to protect my feet from the frigid temperatures. The cold slinked through my torn pants and ripped jacket and settled against my bones. I didn't risk slowing. The heat from the run kept me warm enough that I didn't succumb to the cold. Had I been of only mortal blood, I wouldn't have made it very far. For once, I was thankful for my halfling blood, but it did nothing to stop my legs from screaming in protest. Nix was several feet ahead and stopped dead in his tracks. I almost trampled him.

Faolan was there, waiting, while his guards circled us. Faolan chuckled and shook his head at my sad attempt. But I wasn't trying to escape, not really. I had two options, stall until someone bigger and badder came along and snatched me from him or be killed. Every choice here was between something horrible and death. But anything was better than going willingly to his court, his bed.

"We made a deal." Faolan held out his hand. "Do you really want to break an oath in Elphame?"

"I did not make an oath with you. I didn't say the words. But I did lie to you. Kill me for it," I answered and spread my arms wide for a killing blow. "You can do what you want with my dead body, but there is no way in hell that I'm willingly going to your lands. I'd rather go to your dungeons than spend one night with you. I'd go back to the Golden Court and face the mess I left there before I ever went with you."

"I give you my word that nothing will happen that you don't want to happen," he replied. "The oathing would keep you safe. No one could force you from that safety."

I shook my head. "I won't be caged again."

Faolan reached for me, and I screamed like I had never screamed before. Not even the night of the lashing got this kind of terror from my throat. I would not play his horrific games. I would die before I became his prey for the night. He reached again, and I screamed for help into the emptiness of the forest. My throat cracked under the force of my screams. I reached into my soul and yanked on my Malice, drained and tired and empty. I begged her to help.

"Save your energy. You can't eat them all."

Faolan froze as the sky darkened with wings. Screeches rumbled through my chest. Darkness flowed from the trees and bubbled up from the earth like millions of eels being pushed up through the soil. A thick fog of darkness stood at my back and swirled around us, whipping my hair around my face. A high-pitched squeal flew out from the shadows, creating a wall around me. My little creature hadn't left me. She'd gone for help and brought the darkness back with her. From the fog came hundreds more creatures of all shapes and sizes. The ground hissed and slithered and crawled around me. One man stepped out of the shadows, a warrior dressed head-to-toe in black leather, armed to the teeth with knives of every size.

"Faolan, it has been far too long," the man spoke. His voice rumbled against my chest.

"Great, you called the very person I told you not to call," Nix groaned and hopped up into my arms. "We're all dead now, Perdi. All of us. He is going to eat us."

"You…" I whispered. He was the darkness I'd spoken with so many times before, the darkness behind the wall, the shadows that covered me as I cried, the warmth that blanketed me on so many fearful nights. I wasn't just calling his shadows. I was calling out to him.

"Zephyr, it's been far too long. You will remove yourself from my lands." Faolan stood tall and unafraid. He was even foolish now, with his life dangling before him.

"You do not command me, Little King. You will release the lady and her fellow friend. You cannot take that which is not yours to have willingly." Zephyr reached for the sword on his hip. He steadied his hand, waiting for Faolan to make a decision.

"Neither is she yours," Faolan replied. "You will not strike, or it is war. You do not want a war with the Winter Court."

"You will not drag an unwilling Crow to your land. This is not a discussion. This is not a barter, Little King. If war is what you desire, war is what you shall have," Zephyr answered boldly, with a smile that was all dare and no fear. "It is your choice, Faolan. If you'd like to taste death this soon, it shall be yours—on that I promise. But the lady leaves, either freely or she will step over your dead body on her way past. Make your choice before I choose for you. This will be your only warning. I'm hopeful you disregard it, and I can take your life. For what you've done to her, I'll drag your soul around until the end of time."

I shuddered at the look on his face. His smile was too broad, his lips too red. I pictured him eating the world and still being hungry. But that was what the darkness did. It ate everything. Tendrils snaked out from behind Zephyr, and I finally screamed. The creatures launched themselves at Faolan and his men. Faolan grabbed me in the chaos, and I fought against him. Zephyr was upon him as soon as I realized Faolan had touched me. I ran, with Nix ahead of me and my creature guiding the way. I chanced one look back but saw and heard nothing once I was out of the shadows. I ran until I was blind with tears, and I stumbled.

Nix tried to help me up each time I fell, and he called out obstacles I didn't see. We couldn't stop until we were off Unseelie lands, but the territory was vast and would take days to cross. I couldn't run for days. I couldn't run for hours or even minutes more. Fatigue slowed me to an obnoxious pace, but no matter how hard I begged Nix, he wouldn't leave me behind.

"We rest." Nix led me to a silver maple tree.

"Let's keep going." I didn't want to stop. I needed to get as far away as I could from Faolan, the darkness and the monster who eats worlds. I didn't care how wet I was or that the cold caused me to shiver uncontrollably.

"Perdi, you'll die out here. I don't think you can feel the cold anymore, but your lips are blue. You need to dry off, and you need to get warm, or this is all for nothing when you freeze to death before we get to the Courtless Lands." Nix motioned at the tree. Its roots had long abandoned the ground and crawled above the earth. I followed Nix through the maze of limbs into the core of our wooden shelter, hidden from sight.

Inside was surprisingly warm. The roots had trapped in the heat from the earth and held on to it desperately. Shielded from the elements and prying eyes, it was as safe as it would get for us. I knew it was a short-term measure. Everything we did in this godforsaken land was temporary. The Fae, who lived lives of only the Gods—everything they did was for the immediate, the now. Hundreds of years on the earth, and it all had to be done now. And, currently, I was what they wanted, and they wanted me *now*. They sent everyone at once to hunt me. I tickled their fancy. I was what entertained them in a life so drawn out that they bored quickly of it.

"I need something sharp," I told Nix.

"Why?" he asked, tilting his head and frowning.

I rolled my eyes. "Do you really think I'd harm you?"

"No, but I think you'd harm yourself for me. Tell me why, and I'll find you a stone."

My creature grabbed a stone from the ground and bit into it, cleaving it into two jagged pieces, and dragged over one half, as sharp as any knife. She scolded Nix as she inched past him. I didn't need to understand what she'd said to know she was on my side.

"Thank you," I said as I picked up the stone. "You both had better get closer into the ring I'm about to make."

"Perdi, magick here isn't the same as in the mortal world. It could twist into something none of us wants." Nix didn't budge.

"Probably wouldn't be a bad thing." I smiled, and he grimaced. "Listen... Unless I weave a spell that hides us, we won't make it another day. I won't make it, Nix. I'm too tired to run at a full-out pace. This spell gives us a chance. Now back off before I suck every ounce of magick from your bones and leave you a tiny husk of a gnome."

"Do you understand what this will do?" he asked, and I nodded. "You can't take this back. When you touch dark magick, the dark will touch you back. What happens when it's time to pay for the spell, and we're on the run?"

"We'll never have the chance to run if I don't do this," I answered. Payment be damned. We'd die without the spell.

I dragged the stone over my hand and dripped a circle around my kneeling body. Nix and my creature stood at my feet, inside my circle. I pressed both hands into the earth and searched with my instincts, with the part of me that had been Fae all along. The very magick that held the fabric of Elphame together, the river that ran under the world I wanted to see burn... I sipped from that cup of Fae until I could drink no longer.

I felt the earth shudder beneath me. The life beyond the roots of my refuge swayed at my pull. I could see them, the guards who were searching for me. I watched as they lurked in the shadows, sneering and laughing about the games they'd play with me once their king had gotten all he needed from me and grown too tired of my sight to notice. I listened as they described how my flesh would open for them. I focused on them and pulled from their very marrow their reason to live. This was dark magick, the kind that comes with a cost against the soul. And it would be their souls who would pay the dearest.

I felt the power roll along my body, stolen from the Gate. It wanted out, but it was mine until I willed it to leave. I whispered.

With knot one, the spell has begun.
With knot two, my need is true.
With knot three, so mote it be.
With knot four, I shall take no more.
With knot five, I shall thrive.
With knot six, my veil is fixed.
With knot seven, the spell will not lessen.
With knot eight, this spell is our fate.
With the knot of nine, the cost is mine.
So mote it be.

I fell to my side, pushed my hand through the blood circle and ended the dark spell. I wasn't powerful enough for the spell to last forever, but it would give us time to rest, to find some peace while we sat in hell. It was a needed break from having to run, hidden from the reasons we were running. I curled into a ball and slept. Nix and my creature scuttled about. Their movements were barely noticeable. I stayed in a ball until I could sleep no longer.

I ate in silence and prepared to head back out, but Nix didn't want us to leave the silver oak roots. He didn't want me to see what I had done. But it was my spell, my doing, and I would look upon my actions. I would know, and I would suffer as any should. My soul would pay for what I did. I should see the damage, or I'd never fully understand how very dark this magick could be and why it should only be touched as a last resort.

Every spell had a cost. A balance was restored. Outside the safety of the silver oak, I saw what my desperation had bought on the ground. Six guards lay dead, mere feet from where we'd sought refuge. Their skin was stretched over their bones, paper-thin. I had taken their lives, the force within them. I had eaten their power and left them empty shells on the ground. Those who would have strung me up and tortured me until my body gave out were dead and gone. I should have been happy. I should have been relieved. I should have felt something, but there was nothing. I was as empty as they were. I shed not a tear. I could admit that I wanted to live more than I wanted them to. I knew the guilt would come to me sooner or later. It always did.

"You had no choice," Nix told me once we cleared the forest of bodies and dead earth.

"Yes, I did, Nix. The choice I made is back there, on the ground," I countered. "I'm not saying I'm sorry for it, nor am I reviling it, but I am responsible for it, nonetheless."

Chapter Three

Spell or no spell, I couldn't shake the feeling of being watched, not just seen. Every movement I made was tracked. My skin crawled in warning. With each step forward, my stomach cramped. A sense of dread pressed down on my shoulders. When the hairs on the back of my neck stood at attention, I stopped altogether.

"Nix, something is wrong," I whispered. "It feels like we're marching into the mouth of a beast, to our deaths. It's all over me, the dread. It's awful."

"We're close to the Dark Courts. It'll get so much worse," Nix replied. "It's how they've never been invaded. Would you move in on them, feeling like this?"

I shook my head. "I can't go forward. My skin is about to crawl off. I'm telling you, Nix, that this isn't just a feeling of anxiety. Oh God, it's awful. It feels like a trap. I can feel it all around us. I can feel their very heartbeats."

"And I'm telling you, Perdi, there's nothing ahead of us. I'd know."

I leaned against a tree and closed my eyes. I didn't allow my magick to venture too far from me. I didn't know how far my Malice would cast out around me and couldn't risk breaking my own spell. My magick snuck across the soggy, cold earth like a mouse. From the shadows of the night came the sound of limbs dragging across the forest floor. Trees creaked and branches snapped. Whatever was out there was a hulk of a beast. The snapping of trees reminded me of breaking bones, and my imagination took hold until I pulled back and opened my eyes wide.

"Solas," I whispered as quietly as I could. "He's out there. I don't know where, but I can feel him, and he's sent something to look for me."

"Sluagh," Nix finally answered. "Your spell will hide your energy, but I doubt it will do much to hide your scent. You smell of cold, wet, scared dog."

I left the insult where it landed. I probably did smell of a wet mutt. We bolted through the trees. It didn't matter what direction we went in. Sluagh were everywhere, closing in slowly. The night crawled with creatures, screeching as they grew closer. What had once been a gentle snapping of twigs and brush grew into the complete destruction of the forest around us. They left no rock unturned, no roots intact. I could now smell them—leathery, sweaty and sickly-sweet. They stank of the basement at the Golden Court. I stifled gag after gag, my fear threatening to splatter the ground with my last meal. There was nowhere left to go. It was all for nothing. I'd taken those lives for nothing. I'd broken a piece of myself deep inside—the part that said I would never do dark magick. It was for nothing. I'd stained my very being, only to be taken by the person who'd stolen me into these lands. Solas.

What would he do with me? Had I failed in the only way that mattered to him? Did his friend escape, or had I caused his death? Was he still at the Golden Court? Had I left him behind? Could I do another spell to hide from Solas' hate? Did I have the time? Would I kill even more for another day of freedom? How far would I go after killing them?

I could hear the words Solas had once said to me. *"How many need to die?"*

The panic built inside and stole every breath I tried to take. My chest squeezed at the thought of being trapped. My heart broke at the threat of Nix losing the freedom he fought so hard to take back. We had given it all to get this far, and now it would be for naught. What would happen to Nix and my creature?

"Help." My voice was barely but a hint of a whisper. I closed my eyes and called on the shadows, one of the only friends I had in Elphame. For the first time, I called on that which Nix feared more than Solas. I touched the shadows beneath me and watched as they rolled to life. "Help them. Help Nix and my creature get to the Court of Less."

The blackness crawled up my arms until I could see nothing but swirls of different shades of black. I felt the weight change from thick to thin to thick once more. I rolled onto my back and sucked the air down, starved of oxygen, starved of life. This was useless. I couldn't keep running. It always ended with me begging to run a little farther—but never far enough. I was going to die in Elphame. I just hadn't accepted that fate until now.

I had never gained my freedom back. I could never be free here. I would always be hunted. It was all for nothing. I was a Crow, nothing more, but I could still be less. Soon, I'd find out what it meant to be less than a Crow in a land of creatures who wished for my death. The very nightmares of Elphame hated me and hunted me.

"What would you give for their safe passage?" the darkness asked in return as if it had weighed the choice to help me or not. "Nothing is free, not even for you."

"What do you want?" It was pointless to question it, as I had nothing to give but would give whatever I had.

"I am in want of everything. But what do you, little Crow, have to give?"

I groaned. "Nothing. I own nothing. I have nothing worth anything."

"How tempting an offer you make," it replied. "Little Crow, you could always go with the nightcrawlers. They would take you to Solas. I doubt very much it will be as painful as you think it will be—at least, no more pain than you've already endured."

"I want to believe you, but what if you're wrong?" I asked, but it didn't matter anymore…not really.

"I do not believe I am wrong. You could ask for safe passage to Solas, who will then decide your fate."

"No. I'd rather die."

"You prefer death over an undetermined fate?" it asked.

"Yes," I answered honestly. Death was the only thing I had asked for since being named a Crow. Perhaps today I'd get my wish?

"Odd creature you are. To fight for life and give it away in the same breath. Very well, then. A Crow with nothing to offer presents me with an opportunity to sate a hunger I have. A drop of your soul, a pearl. I will take that."

"Yes," I answered without a second thought.

"You don't care what I plan to do with your pearl?"

"It couldn't be as bad as watching my friends slaughtered—or worse, their freedom taken from them, again." I sobbed at the thought, my words catching in my throat. "My soul is damaged anyway. There isn't much you can do with it that I haven't already forced it to endure." My soul wasn't just damaged. It had been scrubbed over coals repeatedly, kicked, lashed and bruised. The killing blow was dark magick. I took lives. I took futures. I killed for no other reason than to make it one more day. Elphame had picked the perfect Crow. I belonged here, with the other monsters.

"Very well," it answered, and my eyes burst in colors. Fireworks danced behind my eyelids. I felt the pitch-black reach into my chest and pull from me. It hurt the way a broken heart first hurts—devastatingly painful. There was no pain known to man to compare it to. It was just pain that nothing could stop. As soon as it started, it was over. The burning in my chest cooled. I should have been afraid, but I had felt genuine fear before, and this was not a moment worth spending my fear on.

"You taste of pain, other people's blood and home," the dark whispered, then opened itself and pulled Nix in. Behind him was my creature. Before I could tell them of my bargain and what was happening, the darkness rolled inward, squeezing us until I felt my ears pop. One minute, I couldn't breathe. The next, we were touching the ground and were spat out like we tasted awful. The shadows cleared like fog on a windy day, and we stood at the edge of the water, a bank I was all too familiar with.

"What the hell, Perdi?" Nix screamed as he stood off the ground. My little creature shrieked not but an inch from my nose.

"I'm sorry. I ran out of options," I answered.

The three of us turned in a circle. Gone was the dread and the Sluagh. Gone were the eyes tracking us. They were replaced with a calmness of a forest that tired me—a lush forest tucked around us—misty and cool, but not cold. Needled ground, mossy hills and tiny white flowers that shone in the dark lit the way, blanketing the ground. Mushrooms of all shapes and sizes jutted out of cracks in trees and popped up from the moss. The calm breeze carried scents of trees, flowers, clover, lavender, rosemary and fresh water. This spot, this was what I had imagined Elphame to be. It was beautiful, devastatingly so. I breathed in the air and calmed.

"The Court of Less." Nix stood in awe. He looked up at me. "What did you give the shadows?"

"Nothing of any importance, trust me," I answered and knew he'd feel my truth.

I walked in silence. In part because I admired the beauty of the forest, but also because the emptiness inside me had nothing to say. I was numb but felt raw. I was calm, for once, yet I felt unhinged like the next happening would send me over the edge and I'd never come back. So we walked in silence. My creature ate the bugs that came to inspect the invaders of their land, but nothing else came to see who and what we were. It was uncomfortable to not be running or panicking or screaming.

"We can rest in there," Nix said, pointing to a cave barely noticeable from the trees and shrubbery. "We should be safe enough for the rest of the night."

"Should be?" I asked.

He looked up and laughed. "We're in Elphame. This is as safe as it's getting."

Inside, the cave was warm and filled with tiny glowing worms and mosses that flickered with light, and apart from that, it was thankfully empty. Even there, tucked safely away at the back of a cave, shielded from the world, I couldn't help but feel I would never be safe enough. The Sluagh had come so very close. Soon, I knew Solas would come into the Courtless Lands. He was one of the few who came and went where he pleased. Maybe the next time he saw me, he'd kill me for all I'd done at the Golden Court, for all I'd done since leaving. Nothing was free, but I had gotten Nix to safety, and that meant everything to me. It was a fitting end, dying in the back of an old cave, forgotten by the world—another Crow to fall under the touch of Fae.

"I can feel your uncertainty. I'm not angry." Nix curled into my neck. "For what you did to get us here… I can feel a piece of you is missing."

I nodded but didn't want to talk about it. Like him, I felt that missing piece. It was like seeing a painter had forgotten a paint stroke on an otherwise perfect wall. You didn't really notice it unless you lived there and had to look at it every day. I wondered if the feeling of missing pieces would grow over time or if I'd just get used to it? A part of my soul was gone, and whatever was left behind was in ruins. Did it really matter in the end if my soul was tattered and useless?

"What comes next?" I finally asked.

"We find Elswyth, and together, find somewhere to call home for now."

"For six and a half years?" I pointed out. "Can I really hide for that long here?"

"This is the only place you can hide," he answered. "We can find out if there is a new oath or if there is going to be a war. If there is, there is no reason for you to be here. We can get you home."

"Is it awful of me to hope there's going to be a war so that I can leave?" I whispered. I felt guilty for wishing for such selfish things.

"No. We all want to go home, Perdi. What's awful is if you help the dark path along, just to get there. If you really wanted home, if you were really that awful of a person, you'd have asked to be taken to the Gate. Instead, you're hiding in a cave, still in Elphame. You're not awful. You're just scared. So am I."

"Thanks. I think I needed those words more than anything else." I smiled. "He's going to find me here. I don't think there's anywhere I could hide from Solas."

"I know."

Sleep didn't come easy, but fear couldn't win the competition tonight, and I was sucked under.

Chapter Four

I dreamed of the soldiers in the forest, crying out as I took their lives. But in my dream, I looked each one in the eyes and took their lives with my bare hands. Standing behind me was Solas, and I knew before I had even opened my eyes that he stood but a few feet from me. I felt the weight of his gaze on me before I had even woken. He was a familiar feeling, a smell that reminded me he was always nearby. Since coming into this land, he had never been all that far from me…watching, waiting.

Warning or not, my heart still skipped at the knowledge that he had found me. I wasn't stupid enough to think I'd outrun him, but for the briefest of moments, I thought of how easy it would be to drag the life from him as I had with the others. I pushed the thought away. The more I touched darkness, the closer I'd be to losing all of myself. Some things weren't worth a soulless death, not even freedom.

I felt his fingers graze my cheek. "No one gets to touch me without my permission anymore."

"Hello, my little banshee," Solas replied.

"First, I'm not *yours*. Second, I'm not a bloody banshee," I snapped and opened my eyes to him towering over me. In his gloved right hand, he held the same knife I'd stabbed King Aelfdene with. I smiled for the briefest of moments, *poetic justice*. Solas could kill me where I slept with the knife I had used to seal my fate. At least I'd die having tasted freedom once again, by the blade I killed a king with. I could die now and feel satisfied with my end.

"A banshee, or Bean Sidhe, little Crow, literally means a woman of the Sidhe. You are very much a woman of the Sidhe." Solas' grin irritated me. He stepped back and gave me a knowing look. "Perdi, did you really think you could run and I would not find you? There is not a corner in this world, Elphame or mortal, where you could hide from me. Albeit, you've made a considerable effort. The spell was a nice touch. But no one can run from the darkness any more than they can hide from the light."

"I had my hopes," I answered and slowly pushed my cold bones into a seated position. My body objected to each movement. Frigid rock was never an easy rest for weary bones. I twisted my back and cracked my spine into relief.

Solas breathed in my scent deeply and shuddered. "You should have asked the shadows for more than a trip to the Courtless Lands. They could have hidden you from us all."

"Good to know. I'll keep that in mind for next time."

"Don't be so sure of a next time. You killed the Golden King," he said and flipped the blade in his hand, end over end. "With this, of all things. You brought an entire court to their knees with a letter opener. You still have his blood caked under your nails."

"I told you, Solas, I'd kill him before I burned his kingdom to the ground," I replied.

"He deserved it," Nix shouted as he climbed from my jacket.

"This isn't a matter of whether he deserved it," Solas replied. "His death will be avenged, and someone's head will come off for it."

"It was worth it." I smiled, but I was certain that the joy hadn't reached my eyes. "Aelfdene will never harm another soul. He will never take the innocence from a woman again. I'll never regret that."

"And the guards in the forest? Was that worth it, too?" he asked.

"Yes, it was." But not even I believed my words. "Are you here to take me?"

"This is not a social call, little Crow. Why else would I spend days hunting you across the entirety of Elphame, if not to take you?"

"Second time's a charm," I replied. I wasn't surprised. "What about Nix and my creature? Grant them safe passage, and I give you my word that I will leave with you willingly."

"Did you not give your word to Faolan, only to lie and run away?" he asked. "You killed several men with that lie, sucked them dry and left their shriveled bodies for the rest of us to step over. You called on the darkness that had been locked away for centuries to save you. Why would I believe you now?"

"I doubt very much you'd understand why I did it, but just the same, I would do it again and again and again. Because now, there are fewer men who will torture and kill for no other reason than sport. I understand that war is awful—everything about this bloody place is awful—but those who do *that* do it simply because they're stronger and they can. They deserved to die for what I knew they'd do to the next person had I left them alive." I glared at him. "I don't actually care what you think, anyway. I'm just a Crow to you all, with no rights, no voice and not worth protecting."

"Get up. It's time to go." He finally spoke after what felt like hours of him staring and silently judging me for my actions. It shouldn't have bothered me, but it did.

My bravado was gone, leaving desperation behind. "Solas, please, I'm sorry. I'm sorry for all the awful things I said and did. If you want me to beg, I will. Do you want me to grovel? Name your price."

"You're not sorry, though, are you?"

I wanted to lie but knew he'd feel it in his bone as I did. "No. But I want to be, if that counts?"

"No, it doesn't. Now, what are you begging for today? The freedom I told you would never come? I told you if you killed him you'd be hunted."

"Not for me. I don't know how to make an oath or an agreement you'll believe. But I give my word I will go willingly with you, and I won't run away from you. I will not call for help. I will go, and I'll stay for as long as you want, even for all my days. Do with me as you wish. If Nix and my creature are allowed to leave, I will go with you. Tell me how to make an oath, and I will do it."

"And once you're in my lands, you expect me to believe you won't kill my people, as you did to the Golden Court and those who have hunted you, to escape?"

I shrugged. "Everything comes at a cost, doesn't it? If you want me to come willingly—"

Solas interrupted me. "Perdi, whether you come willingly or not means nothing to me. You should know that by now."

"What do you want for their safe passage?" I asked.

"You're willing to bargain for them?" Solas stifled a laugh. "What do you have that I could possibly want?"

"I only have myself," I swallowed hard.

"Did you not just kill men who presumed to have you?" he asked. "Why would I chance that?"

"They wanted me specifically against my will," I whispered and cringed at the thought. My mind raced. My pulse hammered in my ears. "I will give you, me. For them, I will give you my life, willingly, to do with me as you please. No magick, no escape."

"No, Perdi." Nix turned to face me. "You don't have to make this deal."

"You'd die for them?" he asked. "Two little pests?"

"They're *not* pests. Don't say that!" My anger flared. I leaned forward and screamed my words. "They've risked everything to help me, everything. And it was all for nothing. I did it all for nothing. I'm *not* free. I'll never be free. I'll never go home. But they could be. What does it matter if I spend the rest of my life with you or running from hovel to hovel? For them, I would give you my life, or I will die trying to save them from becoming a prisoner somewhere else. They just left one hellhole. I won't send them to another if I can help them."

"We all wear masks to protect our people, but you can't wear yours forever. Eventually, it has to come off. It's as true for you as it is for me." Solas crouched in front of me, repeating what he had said to me, the night

I'd taken my fate from the hands of the Fae and torched the kingdom that caged me.

"Is it time?" Nix asked, looking from me to Solas.

"For what?" I asked.

"Indeed. It's time to take off the masks, little Crow." Solas lifted my chin, and I pulled against his hand. "You cannot bargain for creatures who are mine."

I flinched as if Solas had slapped me. I looked down at Nix. "Solas owns you?"

Nix jumped up onto Solas' shoulder. "He doesn't own me, but I am his, of his court. I was sent to the human world to protect you."

"What?" I muttered. "But you ran from him."

"We ran from everyone, as I told you we would. We weren't safe until we got to the Court of Less. Outside of this territory, Solas couldn't help. We weren't safe until he found us and cleared away those who hunted a little Crow. We kept moving until safety found us," Nix answered. "Like Aoife, we weren't safe until we made it to Solas' territory."

"What?" My stomach flipped, and I wanted to vomit. "Why didn't you tell me?"

"We couldn't risk it. If you didn't fear Solas as everyone else does, they'd have suspected something was up and would have killed you. I'm sorry, Perdi. I had to lie to save us all."

The creature fluttered from my pocket and held her place in front of Solas' face, squealing. Her high-pitched voice made my ears ring. She knew him. That shouldn't have surprised me after seeing her and her kind with the darkness. She finally calmed, landed on the ground in front of Solas and bowed.

"Hello, my little friend." Solas smiled. It was the first genuine smile I had seen on his face since day one. "Orrian, I welcome you home."

"Orrian? Ahh, does someone want to fill me in? Why did she bow to you?" I asked, puzzled. There were too many pieces for me even to try to put any of them together on my own. "You know what? I probably don't even want to know."

"It is customary to bow to a king." Solas smiled, having let the proverbial cat out of the bag.

"I can't take any more of this cloak and dagger shit." My words were barely audible.

"I'll give you the condensed version, as we are running out of time. I am not the only one searching for you, little Crow. The Court of Less is not courtless. It is *my* court, as are all the Dark Courts. It is how I knew exactly where you were. To protect those who have been banished from their courts, those who are too weak to protect themselves, I take them in and give them protection. But to protect them, I've woven lies over lies to keep the lands courtless, from all those who do not know the Dark Courts." Solas sighed, the weight of a thousand lies lifted from his chest. "This little lady is Orrian and certainly not a pest. She has been a constant companion since I was a child. Her people come from the original land of the Fae."

"Didn't you get angry when I fed her?" I asked.

Solas nodded. "I feared for your life, Perdi. Orrian is a fairy, and fairies are deadly little creatures. You saw her come with the darkness and stand against Faolan and his people. They feared her more than what she brought with her, I suspect. She may look tiny, but I would fear her more than any Sluagh. No lie, I would fear for my life if Orrian decided I should not have a beating heart."

"Good to know." I swallowed hard. "But what does any of this have to do with me?"

"When she tasted you, she was looking for someone powerful enough, with enough magick, to help us. She has as much at stake as the rest of us do. If you weren't the one, the Crow who would help us end this, she'd either kill you as a kindness to save you from your fate or abandon us until the next Taking. I feared she'd kill you. Alas, you are the first she has stayed with, the only one she and her people have protected. Finding her still with you, day after day, gave me hope. Seeing her stay in the Golden Court gave me the will to keep going."

"Help you? Why would I help you?" I glared at him. I wished I had taken the iron knife out of the King's chest, because I'd use it on Solas. "Wait. Back up. If you saw her come with the darkness, you were there when Faolan tried to take me at the cabin. You saw?"

He nodded. "Yes."

"You say you want my help, yet you didn't help me when Faolan took me? Why didn't you help?"

"You didn't need my help," he said, as if it were acceptable to watch me be dragged away. "And I needed you closer to my lands. War today would not have been a good resolution for a matter you were handling just fine without me. My people are spread throughout Elphame, I'd never have gotten them home in time and they'd have died."

I shook my head. My pulse was racing in anger. I finally snapped and slapped his face, burning my hand from the force. "You've done *nothing* to help me! You've watched me beaten, tormented and scared. How many times did you just stand there and watch me cry and beg? Hell, you watched me cry myself to sleep for months as I wondered if I'd die the next day. So why are you here now, once it poses no risk to your own hide?"

I reached out to slap him again, and he grabbed my arm. "You were never alone, little Crow. I was there, every single night, watching over you. I never once left you to suffer alone."

"You watched. That's all you did," I countered. "You told me before I left that you had stayed there for me. Why? It's not like you did anything to help me."

"You have no idea what I've given up for you—what we all gave up for you. You don't know how I've helped you, time and time again. Aside from your first night in Elphame, no one touched you because of what I gave for you. Never once did someone step foot into your bedroom because of me. Every mistake you made, I covered it up, risking myself. I paid for it every time. I gave myself, in your place, to those much viler than you can imagine…and I did it for you." His voice was calm, but I could feel the pressure building inside the cave. My ears popped under his energy. "Every bloody prisoner you freed, I told the king that I watched you kill them or saw one of his own people do it. And don't think no one noticed every time one went missing, because they noticed them all. What about the gold you were stealing? I put the suspicion on others and sent countless Fae to the damn prison in your place. Each time you were caught in a lie, I was the one who backed you up and said you were telling the truth. Those who saw through your deceit, who threatened to tell the king of your betrayals, I killed each and every one of them to keep you alive. I can still feel their blood on my hands." He stared at his hands and wiped them on his pants.

"I lied over and over for you and at great risk to my hide, as you put it, and those I planted in the Golden Court to protect you. I risked it all for you. We all did. I risked all my people, everyone, for you, little Crow. It was always for you. You didn't see how badly we all suffered in your name—how many of my people went to the king's bed to keep you from it. My people willingly gave their lives to keep the king's amusement from you. I may be standing here whole, but I left parts of myself and my people in that goddamn court, for you! Don't tell me I came out of it unscathed. None of us did. You, little Crow, are not the only one to pay tithes. We *all* sacrificed!"

I pulled at my wrists, my eyes wide, my hands trembling. I felt his anger crawl across my skin, and I was trapped in a cave with only one way out. "Please, I'm sorry. Please, Solas."

Trapped.

No way out.

Prison.

Crow.

Whatever he saw on my face made him let go and back up.

"Perdi, there's a lot more you need to know." Nix climbed onto my shoulder and rubbed my cheek. "It's okay, breathe. You're not trapped. You're not alone."

I nodded but didn't let down my guard. "Do you plan to kill me?"

"No." Solas frowned. "Perdi, I saved you."

"What?" I laughed. "Look around, Solas. Your idea of saving needs a little work."

"No thanks to you." He smiled.

I dropped my eyes from his. "I had to do it."

"I know, but it still hurts, doesn't it?" he asked. "No matter the 'why' behind what we do, it hurts just the same. Remember that pain. It's the only thing that separates you from the real monsters."

"You were right, you know, when you said I'd learn what true hurt would feel like. You had said I'd use Faolan to measure pain, but this was worse," I mumbled. "What I've done is so much worse."

"In my defense, when I said that, I didn't know you'd suck the life out of those who stood in your way," he countered.

"Why did you save me for this? Why would anyone want to be saved only to endure this?"

"I knew your greatest grandmother of generations ago. Aoife," he answered.

"Yes, I recall you mentioning how feisty she was."

He smiled. "Oh, make no mistake, that she was. But I knew her. I knew her when she became a Crow. She came willingly, a plan of her own making. Darkmore witches were never to be brought into the Sidhe for fear they'd burn Elphame to the ground, but I brought her anyway. I hoped the fears of your line were true, that your line could stop this from happening."

"Why would she willingly come here, of all places? No one is that stupid," I countered then corrected myself, remembering all the mortals who were killed for sport at the hands of the Golden Court. "Well, no one should want to."

"Stupid she was not." Solas' voice was scolding. "She gave her life to the Gate to end the Taking, to end the Seven-Year Crow. We all did."

"Yet, there you were, taking Crow after Crow. For someone who wanted to end it, Solas, you certainly had a funny way of showing it."

"I couldn't end it, so I went to ensure the fewest people died." The heat in his voice lashed the air, and I flinched. "When I took Aoife, a spell was woven into the Gate as she passed through. I felt it. When her feet touched Elphame, she closed the loop on her curse. She cursed Elphame and her line. There would never be another halfling born of this place because no Crow would ever leave Elphame whole again."

"But I'm a halfling," I replied.

"No, you are *of* halfling blood. There are halflings in your line, but neither your father nor mother were Fae. Enough time here, and you will become Fae. You've been here long enough that your halfling blood already calls to Elphame," he corrected me. "Long ago, Fae would go into the human realm and have countless children with humans. It kept the Gate open, with so much Fae blood on that side of the Gate. But the oath ended that. The only other choice the Fae had was to send Crows back with babes already in their bellies. Aoife, her curse ended that. All that was left was the Seven-Year Crow, and eventually, one of enough power to end this all would step through the Gate."

"I'll never leave here," I whispered.

"That, I don't know. I doubt that Gate could hold you if you tried."

I shook my head and huffed. "Why the hell would she curse my line? Me?"

Solas began to pace, stopping every now and again to check outside the mouth of the cave. It felt like we were on a clock I couldn't see. Seeing him of all people pacing had made me nervous. "Centuries before you were more than a spark in the line of destiny, Aoife told me of you. I had to get you to Elphame. You needed to be here."

"Why?" I asked.

"I don't know. None of us ever knew why, only that you would end the Taking. I never knew when you'd come, either. So I went for every Taking in hopes of finding you."

"So, you brought me to the Golden Court?" I sputtered. "To King Aelfdene? Don't do me any more favors, please."

"Would you have preferred I'd brought you to Faolan's court?" Solas snapped back. "I took you to the one place you had a chance of surviving. The only place I could watch over you."

"If you wanted to save me, why not bring me to your court?"

"I couldn't. My court has never made a halfling. I have forbidden it. Even if I had picked you myself, you'd never end up in my court. Crows always go to the court of their line."

"At least Faolan would have killed me quicker," I muttered.

"No, he wouldn't have, Perdi," Nix spoke up. I had almost forgotten he was standing on my shoulder. "Faolan had planned to take you the moment you were born. To what end, I don't know. It is why I was sent to Whitwick, to protect you. But he knew Aelfdene would Take you. How could he not? You're a Wildling. And if he had Taken you from Aelfdene, there would have been a war. Faolan isn't strong enough to fight the entire Seelie Court. You'd have ended up back there. Faolan would have known this."

"I tried to give you the truth. I kept you alive the best I could." Solas' voice had softened. "It was a constant juggling act, and you didn't make it easy."

"Bully for you, Solas. But I'm broken, just the same," I whispered. "What happened to my father?"

"I don't know," Solas answered. "He knew of the plan. He knew if I didn't take you, if I didn't force you to come, Faolan would have. It is why your father didn't fight me to keep you. Your father, who has worked his entire life to keep war from spilling out of Elphame, risked everything to get you to the Gate, to keep you with me, to end this."

"Faolan was molding me, using me." I thought back to the Taking, the moment in my garden. Solas had shown me who Faolan was. "He never did care, did he?"

Solas shrugged. "That, Perdi, I do not know."

"He said he was with Aoife when she died. That he heard her last words. Did he kill her?"

"No. He said that to hurt you," Solas answered. "Elphame teaches us all what hurt is and how deeply it can cut."

I jerked and jumped to my feet. "We need to warn the human realm. The captain of the Guardians, he's going to try to break the oaths and open the Gate."

"We already have, Perdi. We sent a warning to the Guardians we trust." Solas squeezed my shoulder. "Perdi, those you saved in the basement, my people, thank you."

"Are you the fog? Are you the shadows?" I asked, softening my voice as if it were an insult. "Did I just release what will torture my people the next time the Gate opens?"

"No, the fog is Elphame. It's the power of Fae. What you released from the basement is what terrifies the rest of Fae and is much worse than the fog. He's never gone into the mortal world and never will. He's an Aos Si, a Guardian of the Sidhe. The shadows you saw were his, part of him, his collection of souls. He is neither good nor bad, dark or light, Seelie or Unseelie. He is the commander of the entire army of Aos Sí. Many of my Sluagh were locked away with him. The king had been holding them hostage for a great many years. It is how the king had me do his bidding. And as long as I made a spectacle, enjoying what I was doing, my people would live."

"Did you, though, enjoy it?" I asked.

"After hundreds of years of killing, I didn't like it or dislike it. I grew numb to it."

"That's not an answer," I countered.

"No, it isn't. But you don't get to know what haunts the nightmare of Elphame," he answered back. "Now, a king is dead, and his throne was passed to his eldest son, who I do not know well enough to trust. Surely, he is well aware of who I am, but we still need to get you out of here before you're found. Today doesn't feel like a good day for a war, any more than yesterday did."

The world tilted to one side, and the cave began to spin. I swallowed hard. My mouth suddenly wet as if I had to vomit. "My spell…"

"You smell as Aoife did right before she'd use her magick." Solas breathed in deeply.

"I'm not doing magick," I answered. My heart jackhammered. I gripped Solas and staggered. My hand slipped from his arm. I couldn't feel my fingers.

"Payment," Nix finally said and stepped back. "Threefold rule. It's going to be bad, Perdi. The spell used in the basement was hefty, and to hide us, you haven't paid for that one, either. You have a lot to pay for today."

"I'm going to die." I crumbled into Solas' chest as the payment for my Malice ripped through me.

He smelled the air again and grabbed my arms. He breathed in my scent and groaned. "Something is missing, Perdi."

"My pearl..." I mumbled as the darkness wrapped around us and pulled at my mind.

My bones rattled against the gut-wrenching pain coming from within. I screamed, yet no sound could escape the grips of agony. All I could do was suffer silently, thrashing against Solas' hold. He picked me up into his arms, and I felt his warmth wash over me, sending me to sleep. But not even in my sleep would I be free of payment.

I had come this far only to die in the Dark Court with the man who brought me here. It didn't seem fair. It didn't matter about the why behind what he did. I was still here, and my body would remain here long after my soul had moved on. I could only hope my remains poisoned the land.

Chapter Five

I woke up before Faolan could kill me, but I could still feel the cold iron of the knife I had used to kill Aelfdene against my throat. The blade pushed deeper and deeper, and I hadn't struggled to free myself. I could still feel his hot breath against my body, reaching every corner and inch. At my feet were the bodies upon bodies of those I had killed, their blood splashed over my legs. In the distance, I could see Aoife, a look of utter disgust on her face. I lifted my chin, a dare to Faolan to slice my throat. My dream smashed before I could taste the freedom death would bring me. I was disappointed that it had only been a dream, and mercy wouldn't come so easily. The dream was better than reality.

"Perdi?" Elswyth's voice pulled me from a dream I didn't want to wake up from. "Perdi, can you hear me?"

I woke to the feeling of my first time in Elphame, on the barge of the dead. The payment had rolled over every inch of me. My throat was raw as if I had puked up the very pits of hell. My body felt like I had been dragged over hot coals. I felt filled with anguish and empty of everything else. I groaned, scolding myself for expecting anything different. Nothing here was ever gentle.

I scrunched my face and cracked open my eyes, squinting at the brightness of the room. "Els?"

Elswyth looked like a God had been kissed by the sun. Her blonde hair radiated the light coming in at her back. "I didn't think I'd see you again."

I sat straight up in a panic, narrowly missing her head with mine. "Why are you here? Were you found? Where's Solas?"

She placed her hands on my shoulders and pushed me back down. "It's okay."

Nix climbed up the side of the bed. I calmed when his head poked up over the side. "It's okay. You're okay. We're in the Dark Court."

"The Dark Court?" I groaned.

"Solas' home. We're safe here," he answered. "Elswyth was never a slave for Solas. Although what we said was true, he did buy her. She was brought to the Golden Court to help you, willingly. Solas asked for volunteers only."

"Why would anyone willingly go to Aelfdene's Court?" I muttered and relaxed just enough for her to remove her hands.

"Everything I said is true. Solas took me in and helped me. He told me of your coming and where you would go. I went because I didn't want anyone else to suffer. I knew what the Golden Court would do to you, what they've done to everyone who has had the misfortune of being a guest of that court."

"Misfortune, that's one way of putting it." I smiled. "I'm so thankful you made it. What about the others?"

"All but two made it. They passed due to their injuries. They were already on the doorstep of death, but they died free," she answered. "They died in the arms of the others, and they were mourned as they should be. We carried their bodies home to be buried on their lands."

"We did it." I closed my eyes and smiled. I sent my gratitude to the Gods. For the first time, they had answered a prayer. Tears slowly rolled from the edges of my eyes. It wasn't all for nothing. At the moment, the rest didn't matter. How I got to the ending didn't matter. I let myself revel in this one payment given back to me for my suffering. I gave myself permission to be thankful and enjoy this simple moment. I'd never forget what we did before we left. We didn't just save ourselves when it would have been easier and we could have gone sooner. No. We endured until we could take them all, and it was worth the pain in my soul, every drop of it.

"Thank you." I grabbed onto her hand and blinked away my tears. "I wouldn't have made it without you."

"Yes, you would have," she answered, always so kind with her words.

"No, Elswyth. I would have died there if not for your guidance and friendship. I would have been the star of their shows, and I can't even think of what they would have done to me if it weren't for you. I would have wilted and given up. Thank you."

She leaned down and hugged me—a genuine hug, a free hug. "You have given me freedom, of a sort. Had it not been for you, I would never have learned to fight for the life of someone else."

Elswyth helped me fix my pillows and sit up. I grinned at the victory. "I didn't think we'd make it."

Nix propped himself on my pillow. "I never doubted it for a second."

"Not even one?" I teased.

"Okay, when the darkness swallowed us and spat us back out, for those brief moments inside, I thought we were goners," he joked back.

Elswyth carried breakfast to the bed and climbed in on the other side, as we had for so many months before. We ate in bed and pretended the world was right. We laughed, we teased, but we never spoke of the horrors that would unfold around us. In bed, with our tea and cookies and muffins, we could lie to ourselves for those few hours that the nightmares weren't ours. It was the only time we could pretend that it didn't hurt, and we weren't just broken shells of who we wanted to be, who we were before it was taken from us. We carved out happiness where we could.

We shared stories about our escape, skipped the fear and ignored the monsters that had chased us down. Nix laughed at how slow I was. I joked at how huffy he'd become because I couldn't run for hours on end. Elswyth told us she had to punch a nymph in the nose for trying to keep one of the prisoners as interest for the troubles. And as the last strawberry was eaten, I was the first to break the breakfast code and cry. It didn't take long for Nix, my creature Orrian and Elswyth to follow.

Orrian cried for all the times she couldn't save us, for all the times I couldn't understand her and for feeling like she was part of something bigger and better. She found where she belonged, at our sides. Nix translated through his own tears. Elswyth, she cried for the horrors that stained her mind and soul, unhealed wounds unaddressed and fear that wouldn't go away. Around every corner, she'd expected to be taken. No number of breakfasts were going to fix those hurts.

"I'm so sorry, Perdi. I lied to you, and you ended up here anyway." Nix gripped my arm and cried so hard that he shook. "I was sent to you and didn't protect you, didn't warn you in time. Please, I'm sorry. I wanted to tell you, but I was scared the information would kill you."

"It's okay, Nix. I forgive you." I said the words but didn't know if I meant them as sincerely as I should. I had been lied to by everyone, including those I called friends. I was dragged to a land that had left scars on both my flesh and soul. How could I forgive completely when I was still stuck in the nightmare? I wasn't angry with him, but the rest of my emotions were such a jumbled mess that I didn't know where to start the forgiveness.

Nix stood and looked to the door. I knew who it was before he knocked.

"Could you all excuse us?" Solas asked, poking his head in the door when Elswyth called out for him to come in.

"If you need anything," Nix called out on his way to the door. "I'll see you at dinner."

"See you later." I quickly dried my tears and pretended. I was good at that—faking my way. I told myself many times that it would only hurt if I admitted it could. I wrapped myself in anger. It was easier to stomach than anything else. I wondered how long I'd be able to believe that lie before the anger wasn't enough for me to ignore the hurt.

Nix and Elswyth left the room with Orrian flying behind, leaving me alone with Solas. Although he'd come to the rescue eventually, I had months of anger living inside of me. That doesn't just go away. Waking up in a comfortable bed and not being tied to some rack didn't magically make me feel safer or friendlier. After months, I had learned that the other shoe always drops. I couldn't help but ready myself for shoe two.

Solas stepped to the side of my bed and breathed me in. His eyes looked a little sadder at the smell of my tears. It irritated me to know I couldn't hide it from him. More than that, I didn't want pity from anyone. I'd rather he and I went back to needling each other.

"It hurts more after, when it's over. It always does. It'll hurt more tonight when it's dark and you're alone in your head."

"Stop, Solas. You and I are *not* having this conversation." I shook my head, shaking my pain down where it belonged. "I can't. I'm sorry. I can't talk about it."

He nodded. "I won't mention it again. Just know I'm down the hall if you need me."

"Some things never change," I replied dryly. "Are there rules for being here? I don't know the customs of your court. I'd rather not suffer the lash because I didn't know what your expectations are of me."

"*That* does not happen here, Perdi," he replied. His voice edged toward anger, but I didn't feel like it was directed at me. "The only rules here are for the protection of my people. If you need to lash out at someone, leave them alone. I'm down the hall and can take it for them."

"Don't kill your people, noted. Anything else?"

"You are free to leave your room, do whatever you please, save killing my people. I'd urge you not to leave my territory unless you'd like to start a war. You're not a prisoner in the Dark Courts. But, if you leave and go wandering, please let me know and take Nix or Orrian with you."

"Not Elswyth?" I asked.

He shook his head. "Elswyth won't be here much longer."

"Why? Are you sending her away? Now that you're done with her?" I snapped, and even I thought my response was cold. "Do you have some other suffering task for her?"

He ran his hand through his hair and fought the urge to bark back. I watched him swallow his first remark and breathe through it. "Elswyth doesn't belong here, Perdi. She belongs with her people. I've found her a worthy mate who will make her happy."

"You found her a mate? Like she's some sort of farm animal to auction off?" I asked and climbed out of bed. "Are you forcing her to marry? I will not allow you to do this."

He chuckled. "You won't *allow* me? Well, this should be interesting, little Crow."

"Stop calling me that!" I screamed. It felt good to let it out. "No, I won't allow you to sell her off like a piece of fucking meat! You will *not* force her to bed some stranger she doesn't love. This isn't happening, Solas. Mark my words, and allow me to put them in ways only your people understand. If you do this, there will be war. I may be a Crow, but I'll burn it all to the ground. All of it." I winced as I moved toward him, my muscles cramped and sore, but I didn't slow down. Sure, it would take me a few weeks to recover before I plotted war, but it would come eventually. War today or war tomorrow. Either way, I'd find a way to punish him for this.

"Calm down. Before any of this happened, before the storm of Perdita Darkmore, Elswyth asked for my blessing to marry. She is of the old ways. As a member of my court and as her protector, it is customary for her to seek my guidance. And before you start screaming that I picked him, I *helped* her select from noble houses, mates who would honor her, mates *she* selected for herself. Of these suitors, she has spent time with each and, with my blessing, has selected her mate on her own. She put that on hold to save you. Now that you're here, it is time to let her go. It is time she is free. She has earned it and more," he explained, then crossed his arms and squinted an unfriendly look. "Now, you mark my words, Perdi. Elswyth will be free whether you want it to happen or not. Let her be free, or yes, there will be war between us. And no, you won't win on this one. If you try to stand in the way of the life she wants and deserves, you will not enjoy what I will do to ensure it—because it is no different than what I was willing to do for you to taste freedom."

I cocked my head and stared at him long and hard. "I swear to the Gods and Goddesses, and anyone else that's listening, if I find out she's been forced into this, or something bad comes of it, I'll see you dead long before you realize your heart has stopped."

"Of that, I have no doubt. Now calm down and put on some clothes before you catch a chill." Solas grinned and looked down the line of my body. "Though, I wouldn't mind if you choose not to. I enjoy you like this as much as I do in pants and a sweater."

I groaned and covered myself. "Where are my clothes?"

"We had to remove them when you puked on yourself and your nose exploded. There were blood and chunks of your last meal everywhere," he answered and passed me a robe from the foot of my bed. I pulled the robe on and clutched it closed at the top, sitting on the edge of the bed. As Solas grabbed for the door, he turned and smiled. "I'm glad you're here, Perdi."

"I know you didn't have the rights to house the Crow, but if this was where I was going to end up anyway, why didn't you just bring me here to begin with? Why drop me into the middle of hell and wait?"

"You had to leave on your own or it would be war, and I couldn't risk my people on the slim chance you'd help us."

"Why am I here now? And no more condensed version. I want the truth. As you said, it's time to take off the masks."

"I did say that, didn't I?" He smiled. "You're here for the same reason Aoife ended up here and every other Crow who ran here before their time was up."

"Before, when you said you didn't know what happened to her, you said once she fulfilled her seven years, no one saw her again? What happened?"

Solas smiled as if reliving a memory. "She lived out her life, free, here in the Dark Court. I always collected the Crows when they were broken and discarded. I allowed them to live out the rest of their short days here, in mercy and free of harm. Perdi, you need to understand… To keep my people safe, I had to be a monster. That was the mask I chose to wear, and it worked. I had to make sure all Elphame thought I ate them. Even with you safe here, I'll never take that mask off outside these walls. I will always be a nightmare to those who stand against me, and that, little"—he paused when I cringed at what he was about to say—"that, Perdi, is no mask. I will do horrible things willingly to protect my people."

"I'm so grateful that one of us has fond memories of Elphame. Thanks for the rescue—you know, once I didn't actually need your help," I said dryly and waved him off. "I'm sure you have children to terrify and damsels in distress to disappoint."

Solas pursed his lips, swallowing whatever he had planned to say in return, and left me sitting in my new bedroom. Another new home, but not *my* home. I didn't leave my room for the rest of the day. When Nix and Elswyth came with my meals, I ate in silence—not because I had nothing to say to them, but because there were too many things to say and no words to use. My mind was foggy, and each time I opened my mouth, I cried. I was numb from my ears to my toes. Even though I could see happiness around me, freedoms won and love gained, it still felt like, for me, everything gained was not enough, not what I needed. I was still stuck in Elphame with the man who'd dragged me to my fate. It mattered not, the why of it all. I was still here. Broken souls didn't care about the reasons for the cracks.

Eventually, the others stopped coming to my room. It didn't really bother me. I was relieved. I no longer had to pretend or listen to the stories of their lives moving forward while I was stuck in a loop, replaying the past months over and over. A tray was left at my door for each meal, and that was more than enough. I stayed in my room and was thankful it didn't reek of flowers and gold. It smelled of forest, earth and hints of lavender and jasmine when I felt like my blood would boil me alive. I hated Solas for his calming scents and even more for trying to keep me calm. There wasn't enough lavender in either realm to calm the storm brewing inside me. I wanted to tear the room down and scream until the forest was set ablaze with my grief. I wanted something to hurt as badly as I did… Anything. I wanted to unleash it all, but each time I tried to step over that line, my fire would die out, and I'd be filled with calm. I didn't even know who to curse for the forced calmness, so I cursed them all.

Had it not been for my room being the opposite of the Golden Court, I'd have left and taken my chances in the wild, where no lavishness bothered to touch. My room was comfortable but not extravagant. I had everything I needed—not too much, not too little. In my bedroom on the top floor of a two-story house, tucked away from all eyes, I watched life pass by. Minutes eventually bled into days, and I was okay with it, fine with just being there. Hours would mean days, and each would bring me one step closer to fulfilling the oath, and I would return home. I'd probably go mad like the rest, and be put down like the animal I would become, but I would be home. I'd find a way.

One massive window stood at the end of the room with a balcony wrapped around it. The room was simple. It was the view that left me speechless. Solas' home overlooked the forest. It wasn't an estate like the Golden Court, but it was a slice of the world just for him, and it irritated me that he could have something so wondrous and be so monstrous of a man. To be honest, he could live in a castle and I'd ridicule him for that, as well.

From the balcony, I could see for miles and miles uninterrupted. The luxury was in the sights, both day and night. But my favorite of all was the night, when the sky blossomed with stars and a different kind of life. It was a life untouched and untainted. When darkness came, it was brilliant and beautiful and breathtaking—no screams of horror, no begging for life, no hideous laughter, no classical music playing over the sounds of torture. The Dark Court was nothing like I had imagined. I hadn't realized how safe the darkness felt until the first night I saw the night sky. Thousands of shades of black and blue felt like a blanket and not a suffocating force of will. Pain couldn't reach the stars here, and I was envious. I sat for hours, listening to the breeze and birds and nothingness. If I closed my eyes hard enough, I could almost feel like I was home, in Whitwick. Right down to the smells and crickets, it reminded me of my father's cabin.

I had seen every sunset and sunrise since coming here. Sleep wasn't something that came easy. When I closed my eyes, horrors unfolded in my dreams. The nightmares plagued me. They tortured me as if my dreams were nothing more than a prison that I'd brought with me as a souvenir from the Golden Court. I dreamed of Fae being butchered for the amusement of King Aelfdene, me failing, everyone dying in a variety of creative ways and me succeeding only to kill the men in the forest. And when I would inevitably wake in a panic and the room felt like it was closing in on me, I'd sit on the balcony and let the night take it all away on the breeze.

On my fifth night, my nightmares woke me, and I ran. I tore through the manor and pulled the front door open. I had expected it to be locked, for me to be in prison, but it had opened with ease. I ran through the yard and didn't stop. I didn't know where I was going, but stopping wasn't an option. I ran from my nightmares, my anger, my sadness, my soul. My legs couldn't carry me fast enough to escape what ripped my soul apart every single time I closed my eyes. And once my legs gave out, I curled on my side and let the fire breach, charring the grass around me. Solas picked me off the ground and carried me back inside. He didn't scold me for running or for setting his garden ablaze. He simply brought me back to my bedroom, helped me out of the clothes I had taken to sleeping in and pulled my nightgown on. He tucked me into bed and curled behind me until I fell back to sleep.

After a week of screaming myself out of a dead sleep, I broke wide open. It was no different than any other night when I'd woken gripped in fear. Tonight, however, after I dreamed of the Golden Court and the girl I'd vomited on, I woke up screaming and barely made it to the toilet before I vomited as I had that night in the banquet hall. It even tasted the same. I ran to the balcony. I couldn't breathe, and each inhale I struggled for burned as it went down. I gripped the edge of the balcony, willing myself to jump off. When I couldn't do it, I screamed into the night, cursing the heavens for my fate, and cried when nothing inside me changed. I couldn't run away, I couldn't end it, I could only suffer. This was the life of a Crow.

"I'm so sorry." I sobbed into the night. I felt guilty for who I had to be, the monster I had become, to survive that godawful court. It was called the Golden Court, but it indeed was a dark court, the most hideous of places to be. I cursed the Gods for my still-beating heart. "Why didn't you just let me die?"

"It wasn't your time to die." The darkness whispered from the edge of the balcony. I turned, half expecting the shadows to be lounging on my deck chairs, as I had found them so many times before as if they tanned by moonlight. They were never all that far away, especially after waking in terror. But nothing was there. "Hello?"

Before I could call out again, small pieces of rock fell from above. I glanced up and muffled a scream. From the ledge of the house came a hairy tipped tail, followed by wings and a leathered body the size of a wolf. I didn't move. The winged creature dropped to the deck and took a seat on the chair beside me. The chair squeaked under the weight of his bulk. I had seen him out of the corner of my eye several times. At first, I had thought he was one of the Sluagh, but he didn't look quite right. He reminded me of the statues that sat on the church roof back home.

"From up there, I can see all the way to the caves, to my home," he finally said. His voice reverberated through my chest. He pointed a long, clawed finger toward the edge of the forest, to the mountain range. "I do miss it…home."

"Why are you here and not home then?" I asked.

"Sometimes home is where you are needed most," he answered. "Sometimes, you need to leave home in order to protect the place you cherish most."

"I'd like to go home," I said quietly.

"Then what? Will you watch as more are Taken? Have you enjoyed your stay so much that you'd like for others to experience it? Will they have friends to keep them alive, like you do? Or perhaps watch as wars are fought and lost for you being an oath breaker? The sky really is the limit when you think only of yourself." He sighed, and it sounded like rocks grinding together. "The ending you wish for will not be the end for the others. Your freedom will mean the suffering for countless mortals and Fae alike. Fae who have done nothing to you… Their only crime is trying to survive in these twisted lands. And mortals, if they were dragged here, could never do enough to survive here."

"I don't think I care." I finally said the words out loud. "I don't think I care about anything anymore. I feel nothing."

"If you felt nothing, you'd not have woken the forest with your screams. You'd still be asleep, and we'd not be having this conversation." He pointed out a truth I didn't want to hear. "Feeling nothing and not caring? They are not the same. Your pain, thick enough for me to chew on, will pass, and you'll feel once again."

"I don't want to feel anything. When I do, it hurts so badly I can't breathe." I choked out the words. "It's my fault, what happened at the Golden banquets. Because of me, people died. A lot of innocent Fae, who, as you say, have done nothing but survive, died because of me. I watched it. I clapped for more. I don't deserve to be here, to be free." I tucked my knees into my chest and cried. "I killed the king. I stabbed him and didn't want to stop. I can still feel his blood on my hands. It hurts to know I would do it again, even knowing the cost. And now, we're all going to die because of it. They're going to come for me, and everyone is going to die."

"Suffer, perhaps. But death, I'm not so sure," he responded. "You are not in a tempting court to come against. Most would think twice about daring to enter the Dark Courts, even in friendship, let alone battles."

"I should suffer. I've earned it for what I've done. I killed all those men in the forest. I killed them all," I cried. "I could feel them draining. I knew exactly what I was doing, and I kept going until they were empty and would never hunt someone like an animal again. But truthfully, I did it because I was scared and didn't want them to catch me. It wasn't because I was more scared of what they'd do to me. I was scared I wouldn't be free."

"I've heard. All have heard of your journey out of the Golden Courts. I also heard you had very few choices at hand."

"They didn't have to die."

"They most certainly did not, I would agree. But you were not the one to seal their fate. They made the decision to hunt you. You did not go looking for them. They entered the forest seeking *you*, not the other way around."

"It was for nothing, though, because I'm still in this godforsaken place—cursed to become a Crow and help everyone else. But who the hell is helping me?"

"It can be for nothing if you choose—or it can be to save generations yet to come. But, like every step you've taken to this point, you choose what direction you go in. It is up to you and you alone what the rest of your journey will look like. You may have been fated to come here, but now that you're here, it's up to you how it ends."

"What if I don't want to do it? If I don't want to help Solas?" I asked.

"Then you live out your days here and do nothing at all."

"Solas will be angry. Everyone will be angry. I'll have nowhere to go if I don't help him."

"It matters not what they think, only what you can live with. You must walk this path—not they, not I. You must be able to live inside the person you are and will be. If you cannot, then simply, you cannot. Solas would not ask you to leave simply because you cannot do as he or anyone else wishes. And if he should, you would not go alone. You have friends in Elphame. You just need to remember who they are," he replied. "Think on it, long and hard, because when the Gate opens at the end of your seven years, you'll have to watch another Crow step foot onto Elphame soil. Your wings will be passed to someone else."

"I hate my life."

"This? This is not life, Perdita." My name rolled on his tongue like rocks. "You are simply existing right now and doing poorly at it. You can choose to live, or you can choose to cut off those who pray for you to live, each and every waking moment."

"Who prays for me? My friends? The same people who brought me here? The same people who lied every single day to me? They aren't my friends. I have no friends here." My words snapped as if they had teeth of their own. "Who the hell are they even praying to, anyway? A God that left us, or your Gods and Goddesses that demanded our deaths?"

The gargoyle's leathery skin flowed with different colors, all shades of the sky above. His ears tucked back, and he rumbled. "The Gods and Goddesses demand sacrifice for their own sacrifices. You use their magick and energy, and what do you give in return? What do you offer for their power?" His skin darkened with his mood.

"I pay for it," I answered. "They take it out on my hide every single time."

"That, child, is not sacrifice. It is simply a transaction. You pay for only that which you use. Real sacrifice, the kind that stains the world, that is what you know of now. But no one, not even you, has given more than your friends. Your little gnome, Nix? His clan was slaughtered. Their blood spilled for you. He was not there to bury his line. He was with you, always protecting you. He stayed with you, knowing his people were at risk for his coming to you. There is no greater sacrifice than the giving of your history and your people.

And Elswyth? We will not speak of the horrors she endured to get to you and remain with you. She is not and will not be the last to suffer greatly for you.

Orrian was near death when she found you, having given up on hunting food to wait for you, to follow you. She endured great physical pain to remain in a place that spells its lands to kill fairies. Every single breath she took while with you caused her pain.

I won't even mention what Solas had to endure. Those dark stories are not mine to tell, but trust that his pain has been felt for decades. And I do not think I need to name everyone who gave their freedom for you. I think you know full well the sacrifice made in your name. Do not say you are alone when countless have done all they could, given all they had, for your survival. And you thank them by slowly allowing yourself to fade. You honor them not by allowing yourself to wither and die. If your slow death is what you wanted, you could have stayed in Alfheim and died without risking so many for survival you don't even want."

"I didn't know," I whispered and regretted my hostilities toward him. I let out a breath I didn't know I had been holding deep in my chest, finally ridding myself of the vise squeezed around my ribs.

"How could you know? They are your friends. Why would they remind you of what you cost them, what they paid to ensure you lived?"

"I don't know how to live anymore."

"One day at a time. It will not be easy, and it will hurt more later than it does now. As each day comes, another raw layer of pain will need to heal. There is no greater pain than that of a war that must be won within our soul."

The creature stayed with me on the balcony until I calmed. And when I rose to return to bed, he saw my hesitation and came with me. His wings dragged on the oak floor behind him. He climbed onto the bedpost and watched as I inched into bed under him. His tail hung down, and I curled my hand around it. I listened to his claws dig into the bed frame as he balanced, the wood cracking under his force.

"I, like you, miss home," he said. "But home is wherever I'm needed, and I'd never go back if it brought them risk."

"Do you think I'll ever go home?" I asked.

"I think you'll find your home. Where that is, that is for you to decide," he answered. "But know this… Home isn't a place you can find. It is wherever your soul can rest in peace."

Chapter Six

I didn't remain in my room in the morning. I wasn't ready to face anyone, but I also wasn't prepared to live out of one room. I washed and dressed in simple cotton pants and a shirt, with slippers built to glide. My light charcoal clothes were nothing like the stuffy attire I had been forced to wear in Aelfdene's court. Upon closer inspection of my wardrobe, there wasn't a single thing that would scratch my skin or glittered like a gem. Nothing would feel like I was being strangled by fabric. There was an unusual amount of leather pants and jackets, but one touch said it would feel nice against my skin.

I finally saw myself in the mirror, something I had avoided up until that point. I feared what I would see or wouldn't have the courage to look at. When I met my eyes and was able to hold the stare, I saw what the months had done to my soul. The butcheries I had witnessed, the macabre revelries I had joined, had eaten me to my bones. Inside my head was a dark place to be, but it was finally quiet. The practical part of me still functioned just fine. Survival instincts were more difficult to kill than hope. My eyes stung with unshed tears. I willed the tears to come, to break free. But they, like me, had grown stubborn and wouldn't breach their walls. And no matter how hard I tried to take the contorted look from my face, forever frozen into a sleepless and painful expression, no smile would come.

One foot in front of the other, I told myself as I stepped out of my bedroom for the first time since coming here. My heart thumped in my chest. I wandered the hall from my bedroom, down the stairs and counted every potential escape. I tried each door on my way by. No door was locked, no window latched shut. Stubborn windows had me panicking until they opened. The very notion that I could be trapped in one of the rooms made my stomach ache until they finally squealed open.

Solas' home was not what I had expected. It was breezy but warm, from the temperature to the décor. Each room smelled of vanilla, lavender and herbs that made me think of Orrian. When I climbed down the stairs and onto the main floor, my stomach was in a knot. From the corner of my eye, I watched the shadows in the corner of the room slink down the wall. Since finding them in my bathroom in the Golden Court, they weren't too far from me. The anxiety in my stomach lessened once I saw them, enough for me to keep moving forward. I followed the scent of breakfast.

I stepped into the dining room…if one could call it that. The back end of the room was a massive solarium overlooking the forest through floor-to-ceiling windows. Solas looked surprised to see me. He jumped from the table and stared, unsure of what to say or do.

Any movement from him, and I'd have probably bolted. We stood frozen and stared at each other. Neither of us blinked or even breathed. Eventually, he stepped back from the table slowly and showed his hands were empty. I watched his throat bob as he swallowed hard. My stomach swirled with butterflies.

"Are you hungry?" he finally asked. "Eat with me? Or I could leave. Yes, sorry. I'll leave."

I could hear the worry in his voice, the desperation for me to sit with him. I squirmed in my loose shirt and pants, feeling them twist against my waist. The weight loss hadn't been as noticeable until now, under his stare.

"No, stay. This is your home," I answered and moved toward the table. My stomach cramped, both with hunger and nervousness.

"How are you feeling today?" he asked.

I smiled a weak and faded response. Finally, I shrugged and took a seat at the other end of the table. "I don't know. Empty, I suppose. Angry. Broken. Hungry. Happy I'm not wearing a dress or needing to put salve on a new itchy rash."

"It's understandable. You've been through a lot. If you need anything at all, let me know."

He filled my plate. His hand vibrated the serving spoon against the porcelain. It reminded me of chattering teeth. I cringed at the thought and felt a small flash of heat from his body. Anger flared in his eyes as he took his seat at the other end of the table.

"Have I done something wrong?" I asked quietly and shrank a little in my seat. I was torn between wanting to be sick and bursting into tears at the thought of doing something wrong, as though I were back in the Golden Court, carefully weaving lies, and I was about to be caught as a traitor. I stood, trying to will my feet to move forward. "I should go. Sorry… I didn't even ask if I was interrupting you."

"No. Stay. Please sit. You've done nothing wrong. I promise. It's just that I can smell your fear," he answered, his eyes still burning. Around him, I could see an aura of darkness, churning and dancing in a wind I couldn't feel. "You're not the person I'm angry with. Please, eat. I'll calm down, I promise. Just know that it isn't you that sparks this feeling inside me."

I sat slowly, my eyes on him and the only door out of the room. I flinched each time his anger rolled out, but I calmed a little once he ate it back down. I swirled my food around on my plate, not caring what he had given me to eat. It would all be tasteless anyway. It always was. I noticed he had an obscene number of potatoes on the table, cooked in every imaginable way. I didn't think I had ever met someone who loved them this much.

I thought of small-talk topics, anything to cut the uncomfortable silence, but didn't want to talk about what ate at me day in and day out. More importantly, I didn't want to talk to *him* about it. I didn't see him as a friend, an ally…not yet. Trust, most definitely not. I almost died because of the last man I had trusted. I doubted very much that Solas would be another name I'd willingly add to that list. It didn't matter to me that he had stayed in the cursed court for me. Not yet, anyway.

"Do you like your bedroom? Do you need anything?" He got the hint and changed the subject to meaningless small talk. He leaned back in his chair, sipped his coffee and watched me.

"Yes, I do. No, I don't need anything, but thank you," I answered and instantly felt awkward in my own skin. "The view is spectacular."

"Indeed, my room is at the other end of the hall. The backside of the manor has the best views," he answered. His gaze, hot and heavy, didn't recoil from me. He had been the only one, since coming here, who didn't flinch when I looked at him. It made me uneasy, and I moved in my chair.

"Do you live here alone?" I finally cut through the awkward silence.

"Yes, although I'm rarely alone. The guard is always here, Sluagh come and go and there's the odd messenger. Why? Has someone bothered you?"

"No, just wondering. Am I really free to come and go?"

"As I said, you're not my prisoner—but you are hunted by the majority of Elphame. I'd feel better if you took someone with you when you went out—or at least let me know."

"They'd be stupid to come here for me."

Solas nodded. "I'd agree, but some will need a reminder."

"What will happen if they come for me?"

"They die, like any other who has ever stepped foot to my door, uninvited."

I sighed. "No one should have to die for me."

"It will be their choice—not mine, not yours." He smiled. "When you play dangerous games, you win dangerous prizes."

"Perdi!" Nix's scream tore through the halls and into the dining room. "Solas, Perdi is missing! Perdi!"

"Nix," I called out from the dining room.

Nix ran in at full speed and skidded across the floor to my feet, scrambling to come to a stop. He grabbed onto my leg and squeezed. I could feel his heart pound against me. "Oh, thank God. There's a gargoyle in your bedroom. I thought it ate you. I tried to climb into his mouth after you. Orrian is still in there. She's threatening to dig you out through his belly button."

"How did you get a gargoyle to come inside?" Solas asked, an amused look replacing the rage that had refused to back down completely.

"He's been here all week, above my patio." I shrugged. "I don't know. I wasn't having a good night and was out on the deck. He plopped down beside me, and we talked. He walked me back to bed."

"Did he talk back?" Solas asked and leaned forward, putting his coffee down.

"Yes. Why wouldn't he talk back?"

"Huh, what did you talk about?" He asked.

"*Things*. He just listened, really," I answered with no great detail, avoiding the question as best I could. Solas was no fool. I woke the house every night with my screaming. But he didn't get to have my nightmares or my truth.

"He?" Solas asked, and I nodded. "A male gargoyle?"

"Is there some significance in that?"

"It's a rare thing indeed when males are found outside of the caves, away from their lands. And to have one willing to talk is even rarer. It is told they only come for war."

"Who is at war?" I asked.

"When is there not a war?" Solas' answer was very Fae.

Nix hopped onto the table and dragged his small chair and table down to my end and sat at a place setting small enough for him. I thought it was sweet. He had a place of his own. It made me smile, the thought that Solas made space for everyone.

"Gargoyles are said to bond with only one and will protect them against all evil. The Gargoyle said he slept in your room, over you, protecting you. He's going to be hard to get rid of now," Nix piped up, serving himself breakfast. "You think fairies are pests, just you wait. They make me nervous."

"Aren't you going to go tell Orrian that I'm fine?" I asked.

Nix shrugged. "No. She'll figure it out when it eats her and she can't find you in there. Don't worry. He'll spit her out. Fairies are hard on the stomach."

Solas chuckled and leaned back in his chair. "You make friends everywhere you go."

"I'm a witch, Solas. It's part of my charm."

"Many charms indeed. I'm happy you've joined us today." Solas lifted his cup in salute. The cup looked incredibly small in his hands.

"What happens now?" I asked, which was the main reason I left my bedroom. I needed to know what was coming for me, what my future would hold and what bitter fortunes were mine to be had.

"Whatever you want to happen is what happens now," he answered, as if it were that simple.

"I killed a king, Solas. What will happen to me? I doubt very much they'll let me choose my own fate."

"His son claimed the throne before the Aelfdene's body cooled. I don't even think he even tried to save him. Although, from what I saw, there was little to save."

I risked a glance across the table. "Should I say sorry?"

"No, and you shouldn't be. You'd probably be the only one who was sorry about it. His fate was a long time coming," he answered, and I felt the rush of anxiety fade. "I'm guessing the son will seek vengeance once he's collected his army. He'll need one hell of an army if he's going to come to these lands for you. He knows I have you, which would put you under my protection. If he's smart, he won't bother. He will be a new king with few allies. I don't know if any other court would risk coming here with him."

"What does that even mean, Solas? Stop beating around the bush and just talk to me in plain, non-Fae language."

"He'll either let it go, thankful his father is finally dead, or he'll wage war." Solas poured himself another coffee, calmly, as if he weren't talking about the risk of war. "Young kings are unpredictable. They always want to be bigger and better than the last king. The only way to be bigger than Aelfdene is to slaughter his way here. A war against the Dark Courts would be the only thing Aelfdene hadn't done in his long rule. So, in plain, non-Fae, language, he will either try to kill you or he'll be too scared of me to bother trying. If he comes into my lands, it'll be a bloodbath of Golden soldiers."

"Explains why the gargoyle came to my room." I groaned and felt myself closing in. Guilt tightened around my soul. "Enough people have died already."

"If I can help it, no one shall. These lands haven't been successfully invaded since my father built them with his bare hands. They've tried, but no one who has come has ever lived to talk about it," he answered and put his coffee down. "The monster I've shown Elphame is the monster they expect me to be and what I've used to protect my people for centuries."

"Aoife told you to bring me here, but did she tell you what I would need, how I would stop the Taking?" I asked.

"No," Solas answered and turned his attention to the doorway. "She was very selective with the information she'd share, always cautious not to steer your destiny."

"Bring her to see your grandmother." A man's voice echoed in the room mere seconds before he followed it in. A man—no, a warrior—walked into the room and instantly filled it with his presence. Dressed head to toe in weapons, tall as Solas but bigger somehow, he took up more space than needed. His white-blond hair was tied back in a single braid, but small wisps of hair floated around in a wind I couldn't see or feel.

"You…" I whispered. The shadow man, the man who'd rescued me from Faolan, stood in Solas' house as if he were at home.

"Zephyr, it has been far too long." Solas stood with a smile. Unlike Faolan, Solas was happy to see the man. "Why didn't you come the moment you were released?"

"After that long in a dungeon, I had my own oats to sow. Thanks to your little Crow…" he started, and I stood at the table.

"Don't ever call me that again." My lips curled into a snarl. That one word triggered my defenses, my anger. I slammed my fist into the table. "I am no one's bloody Crow."

"My apologies, my lady." He nodded and tipped his head. He turned back to Solas with an ear-to-ear grin. "I told you she'd come for me. Who is the fool now, Little King?"

Solas glided to Zephyr with a smile, his arms open for a hug. The hug he gave came in the form of a punch hard enough to send Zephyr into the wall, cracking the granite. Solas and Zephyr exchanged blow after blow until Solas had him pinned, face down, his arm wrapped around Zephyr's throat and Zephyr's arm crooked in a perilous position. One wrong move, and I would hear bone snap.

"Give it back, Zephyr!" Solas yelled.

With a bloodied face, Zephyr grinned. "Whatever do you mean, My King?"

"You are the only Soul-Eater in all of Elphame, and Perdi is missing a pearl. Spit it out, or I'll dig around inside your gut until I find it."

Zephyr pushed up from the floor and sent them both into the ceiling. The fight, it seemed, was not over. Their hands and feet were too fast for me to track, but the room echoed with the sounds of flesh against flesh, bones crunching and snarls that sent shivers down my spine. They were two animals entangled until one would finally die.

"You know I can't do that, Solas. It is mine to keep. She gave it willingly, an oath."

Solas grabbed Zephyr by the throat and lifted him off the floor. "You'll give it back now, or I will eat everything you love."

Zephyr barked a loud laugh and twisted his body to grab Solas from behind. "There is only one I care for, and you'd die before you touched her. I will burn your cities to the ground for even thinking of harming her, just to prove that I will come for you next."

The room filled with shadows that danced along the walls. Solas' body darkened. It looked like the very night sky moved just below his skin. "If your shadows so much as touch me, Zephyr, I will fucking kill you."

"You will try, and you will fail," Zephyr responded. "And I will schlep your soul around until the end of days. That's a long fucking time, with a pissed-off Soul-Eater, for you to contempt your existence."

"Stop!" I yelled, and the room froze in utter surprise and stillness. Solas let go of Zephyr's hair, and Zephyr let Solas' hand fall from the clutches of his teeth. "I thought you two were friends?"

"We are," they said in unison.

"Then why are you fighting?" I asked, watching each look from me to each other and back, confused.

"This is what we do," Zephyr finally spoke, shoving Solas off him and both jumping to their feet. "We fight, and we screw. It's what we do."

"How poetic." I shook my head, and Zephyr wiggled his eyebrows.

"Perdi, the shadows are part of Zephyr. He took one of your pearls, a drop of your soul. He can give it back willingly, or I will cut it out of him," Solas said, the words more as a threat than an explanation. He loosened his shoulders, ready to fight once again.

"Zephyr, what will you do with my pearl?" I asked.

"Nothing, I collect them," he answered.

Solas growled a warning. "Like hell you do nothing. He is tied to the owner of that pearl, always. You've seen his darkness, his shadows. Those are his pearls—souls, Perdi. Do you want your bloody soul being tugged all over Elphame just to come at his every beck and call?"

"I don't do that to my pearls, only the souls I punish," Zephyr countered. "I'm not a monster. Close, though."

I moved to Zephyr's front and extended my hand to him. Black tendrils of magick moved from my hand to his, calming him. "Thank you for helping me. It is a pleasure to meet you."

"We've met many times before," he reminded me and stared at our connected hands. He frowned for a moment. His eyes were heavy on mine as my magick touched his very soul. I felt him fight it at first then relax into the safety of it. "I knew you'd come. When they took me, I knew it would be you who would free me. I've always known you'd come."

"Yes, but I didn't have the chance to stop and get your name," I answered. When his shoulders relaxed and his breathing returned to slow and steady, I climbed up his front and wrapped my hands around his throat. "Give it back!"

The thought of a Fae being linked to me, knowing my every movement, made me panic. I'd be trapped in his darkness, a piece of me never truly being free. I clawed at him as he struggled to pull me off without hurting me. His movements were careful, too careful. Mine were far from cautious. I would dig the pearl out of him through his chest if I had to. I wouldn't be trapped. I didn't leave one prison to be caged in another.

"A little help, Solas?" Zephyr called out as he tried, and failed, to peel me off him. He slapped the top of my head twice. "What the hell is wrong with you? Stop biting me."

"Nope. You got yourself into this. You figure out a way to get her off you," Solas answered. "Good luck. And a word to the wise… I wouldn't take my eyes off her. She'll brain you a good one."

Zephyr pulled me from his chest and held me out in front of him like a spoiled child. I kicked and reached for him, but he held me out farther. When I knew I'd never get another chance, I whistled. The room burst with little creatures. Even in my darkest hour, they were always close by, always waiting. They zipped back and forth, scrambling over his exposed skin, ripping at him with razor-sharp teeth. Nix crawled up his leg to his face and bit his cheek.

Zephyr dropped me and picked Nix from his chest. He lifted him to throw him and stopped himself. He put Nix down as though he were glass. Once Nix was safe from Zephyr, I kicked the side of his knee and took him down to the floor. Before he could move, I straddled his chest. I grabbed him by the collar and screamed, inches from his face. "Give it back, *now*. You don't get my freedom, Zephyr. You don't get to trap me forever! I will hunt you to the ends of this goddamn realm, and I will eat your fucking s…."

Thunder rocked the room and darkness swirled. Wind ripped at my hair. Zephyr's eyes zeroed in on me, and he snarled. I didn't flinch. I snarled right back. Darkness, deep from within my Malice, burst to meet his. The creatures were blown from us, and Nix rolled away. Zephyr grabbed me, pulled me to his chest and we were gone, behind a wall of shadows. One moment, we stood in Solas' dining room, and next, we stood in an empty forest. I sucked the energy from the air and balled it into my fists.

"You will eat what, little Crow?" Zephyr smirked, and I said nothing. He pointed at me and let his careful mask melt from his face, which said he wouldn't hurt me. All that was left was a promise of pain. "If you ever touch me with your magick again, I will end you. My soul is not for the taking. Do it again, and you will feel all kinds of hurt. There's no one alive who could stop me."

"You may cause me *pain*, you may break every bone I have but I will eat your fucking soul, Zephyr, before I let you *hurt* me," I screamed at him. The words came out of nowhere. My stomach rolled with anger. I was stuck between wanting to reach for all his pearls and clawing out his eyes.

With my rage came my Malice, begging to get out. It wanted to tear up and down his mind and take it all from him. I could feel her knocking on a door I'd never be able to close once opened. She nudged me, coaxing me, convincing me. She was starved. I had given her a taste of drinking true power, of eating down the souls of the soldiers, and she wanted more.

"I smell your magick, Perdi. I can taste it on the tip of my tongue." With a cocky grin, Zephyr lifted his hand and waved me forward. "Take your best shot, little Crow."

"Don't call me that," I snapped and charged at him.

He blocked each strike with ease, like swatting a fly. He grabbed both of my fists and shoved me backward. "You are the very night, black as a Crow. You were born to eat worlds. Yet, you fight with your anger and not with your head, not with the power resting in your bones. You're all rage and no skill. You are the cleaver of lands, the very blight we brought into our homes. In war, when the fear others have of you is your only tool, use it to your advantage. You say you will eat my fucking soul, so convince me you can."

I screamed wordlessly and attacked again. And again, I failed.

"You are trying to muscle someone who is three times your size, one hundred times your strength and older than the written word. You will never win that way. Use what you have, not what you *wish* you had."

Tendrils of my Malice snaked from my body. But there was no focus, and they were wild and free. Zephyr lifted his hand, palm up, and pulled the darkness into his hand, crushing it as if it had never been. He waved his fingers, daring me to continue.

"I eat souls, and your Malice is nothing more than an extension of your soul. It was delicious after such a long fast." Zephyr still smiled, and I still wanted to wipe the look from his face. He watched me flex my fists. "You will need to do better than that if you wish to stand against the likes of me, little Crow."

"Go to hell!" I cried.

"We both know a thing or two about hell, don't we?" he called out, moving from left to right and circling behind me. He kicked the back of my knee, and I went down. "Hell isn't a place we can simply go to and leave as we please. It is the pain we live with—a place we bring with us everywhere we go. Right now, we are dancing in yours, and I could vacation here."

"Up yours." I stood and rolled my shoulders. "You don't know me. You don't know anything about me, Zephyr."

He shrugged. "Maybe, maybe not, but I know the look in your eyes. I've had the same look. I've felt the same shame and pain and hurt and hate for myself."

I swung and connected. "I doubt that very much."

"Your survival doesn't mean those who died meant nothing. Becoming a monster doesn't mean you are one. It means you didn't want to die." He grabbed my wrist, twisting it until I turned, and he pulled me against his chest and held me there. My heart pounded against my bones while he remained perfectly calm. "The feeling of being trapped, being anyone's next victim, being nothing more than meat for the birds… The feeling of never tasting freedom again… That fear, that terror, I know it all too well, Perdi. Try living that for decades, centuries."

I shook against his chest. "Let me go."

"The only difference between you and me is that you are not alone," he answered and pushed me from his body. "I was, and I listened to my people die, every bloody day. I listened as they called out for me, and I couldn't help them…"

"I tried to save them!" I burst with anger with a wind that pushed him away from me. The rage from deep within me splintered the trees and shook the rocks free of the ground's grip. The rain poured from the sky, and I finally screamed. "I couldn't save them all. I tried. I would have given anything, *anything*, to save them. But I was too late."

"It wasn't your job to save them. It was your job to survive." He blocked each blow I threw. "I was there. I know you tried, and that is more than anyone could ask of you. It was more than anyone else did."

I had done everything I could do to save as many as I had been able…but failed. I'd watched countless nights as they were marched from the dungeon, through the banquets and forced to dance for the Fae. I'd listened to them scream and beg and couldn't help them. I'd ripped my soul to pieces every night, thinking I could have done something, I *should* have done something. Again and again, over and over, I'd watched and done nothing. I wanted to live more than

I wanted to do what was right. My need to survive meant more to me than their need to survive.

"They didn't deserve to die!" I screamed. "Faolan took everything from me. He took it and left me for dead. He sold me into hell. That bastard killed me over and over, every night. I died inside because of him. I'm a shell, dead inside."

"It wasn't your fault," he repeated.

"You went there, waited for me and watched your people die, and now all you have is me, a broken Crow. I can't help anyone anymore. I don't want to."

"I waited for you. You freed me so that I could free you. But you've done enough now."

"I can't do this. They broke me," I cried. "They took everything good I had and burned it away. I hate you all, all of you! I may have a pulse, but I'm dead inside! I have nothing left to give this cursed hellhole."

Finally, my knuckles hit flesh, and it startled me. I looked at my hands then at Zephyr, who was bloodied. He grabbed me with liquid speed and held me against his chest, my arms crossed in front of my chest, under the weight of his hold.

"It wasn't your fault. You did your best," Zephyr repeated, and I struggled against him.

Trapped.

Owned.

Prisoner.

Monster.

I dug my nails into any flesh I could grab with all my might, but he still held me as tightly as my panic. I raged in his arms and let that part of myself open up, the part I locked away for fear I'd be killed, just like my mother. I let my darkness out. This time it was focused, directed solely at Zephyr. It was nothing like his shadows, but it still made him take notice and loosen me slightly. I tried to drop, but his hold was a vise I'd never simply walk away from unless he willed it. Zephyr snatched my dark cloud from above him, small enough to fit into the palm of my hand and squashed my pathetic attempt into nothingness.

"Do your worst. I can take it," he whispered in my ear. "Go ahead. There is nothing you can do to me that hasn't been done before. For you, I'd suffer."

Murderer.

Worthless.

Halfling.

Crow.

"Give it to me to carry. I can taste your pearl, little Crow, and I would do anything for your pain to stop, even for a day."

"My soul hurts. I just want the pain to stop. I'm not like the rest of you. I can't just bounce back from hell as if nothing happened," I cried and sagged in his arms.

"You are the only one who expects this much from yourself."

"Give it back, Zephyr. Give me back my pearl."

"I can't give it back," he said the moment he let me go.

"You don't get my freedom," I cried. My small sob turned into a gut-wrenching scream. I dropped to my knees and pounded the earth. "No one gets to own me. I'm not a thing."

"I don't have nor want your freedom—and I'd kill anyone who tried to own you."

He knelt beside me as I came undone. He said nothing as I screamed my frustration and sadness into the vast nothingness of the forest. The shrill of my pain sent birds and creatures scattering. I cried until my throat cracked, and nothing was left. Finally, I dropped to my side and rolled onto my back, staring up at Zephyr and beyond, to the tips of the trees that kissed the sky.

"Why would you ask for my soul?" I asked.

"Because I need it," he answered.

"Why? It's a broken mess."

"When you were brought as a Crow, you called my shadows from me. It was with your call that they tasted freedom for the first time in a very long time. Through them, I could see you. I was curious who you would be. I could feel you, curled in the cell, begging the Gods and Goddesses for survival." He closed his eyes and cleared his throat. The cells weren't a place to speak of lightly. "Little bits of my shadows could come and go, not bound by a spell against Fae. But with you, they felt your call, and I was curious who would have that power. My shadows hadn't felt a call before, nor had I. It was an unusual sensation to feel a person's need so deeply. But then I found you, a Crow who can call darkness. *The* Crow who would help me, and in turn, I would help her. And there you were, in that prison, and I couldn't get to you. Your body was broken, but your will to live wasn't. You begged for death, but you weren't ready to die, not truly."

"Yes, I was," I countered.

"Then why didn't you throw yourself off the manor balcony? Why didn't you drown yourself with the nymphs? Why didn't you run into the darkest parts of the forest, where God-knows-what lurks? You could have simply bled yourself until you died. You watched countless people die at their own hands. You could have simply followed them. Hell, if you had asked Orrian, she would have given you poison enough to end it all. Your options to end your life were endless in a court built on death," he answered.

"What you were looking for was an escape, not death. And each time I found you, your soul was still fighting. *You* were fighting. You were willing to die, but only to save others, not just to end your suffering. When you bargained for Nix and Orrian, I took your pearl because I knew, at that moment, you were ready to die, for no other reason than to taste the end. You wanted death for the very first time since coming to Elphame. You wanted me to ask for your life, not just to save your friends but to finally end your suffering. I took your pearl so I would always find you. I took it so I could save you when you needed saving most."

"Can you truly not give it back?"

He shook his head. "Even if I wanted to—which I don't—I can't. It is as much a part of me as my heartbeat is. That pearl is with me until your last breath."

"Why wouldn't you want to give it back?"

"Because I'm scared of what you're going to do to yourself, to end the pain."

"I'm not going to kill myself, if that's what you think." I snorted a laugh that morphed into another frustrated scream.

"But you're not going to live, either, are you?" he asked.

I didn't have an answer. But I also didn't owe him an explanation. "What did you do with it? Is it really in your shadows with the others?"

"No, I didn't put you there." He patted his stomach. "I ate it."

I laughed, surprised at his answer. "You *ate* it?"

"I'm a Soul-Eater. What else would I do with it?" he asked. "My shadows are souls of those who deserve to live forever, to be trapped forever. They do not deserve freedom. Locked in eternal darkness, they have no will of their own."

"Do you own me now, as you do them?" I asked.

"No. I didn't take your pearl as a punishment," he answered softly. "It lives within my own soul. I will feel you, during your fear and grief, like last night. I thought you were going to jump from that balcony. I was waiting below to catch you. I felt your pain and hurt and sorrow. Still, I feel it. It coats you like thick perfume."

"I can't even die here in peace." I scowled. "What does it feel like to you?"

"It feels like waking up and being the only one alive in a strange world—to have woken up and everyone else is gone. Those I love are gone. And now I must walk the earth, broken, enduring it all, alone."

"That's pretty bang-on, Zephyr."

"You're not alone," he reminded me.

I smiled weakly. "Pretty to think."

"Your fear blinds you."

"Wouldn't you be scared?"

"No, I wouldn't. Though, I was created for this. You weren't. But, even in your greatest moments of fear and pain, you thought of others and their suffering. You risked your freedom and life to save those no one thought worth saving. You risked your life to save mine. I watched, at the end in the Golden Court, when you looked back to make sure everyone had made it out. I watched at the end of the tunnel when you knew you were being hunted. You stopped running for your life to dig a pixie from the mud. You came back for Solas, the only one there who didn't need to be rescued. You wasted precious moments to keep saving others. I knew you'd have gone back into the basement for anyone else who wanted their freedom. Thank you, little Crow." He winked. I knew he'd never stop calling me that.

"You're the friend he said was trapped there. Solas told me you went willingly. Why would you do that?" I asked. "How did you know I'd free you?"

"To save my people from a war that I knew would take the lives of more than it was worth. I traded my freedom, knowing you'd come."

"Do you see the future?"

"No, but I do have an idea of my fate. Yours is tied to mine, and your pearl tastes of home. And if we ever wanted this to end, I knew I'd have to sacrifice as the Crow would, or why would she choose to come to us if no one else paid in the same way as she. You couldn't be the only one to give their freedom, to be cut off from their home, to suffer, to feel pain and hurt and feel alone in a world that bets on their death." He smiled, and it softened the terror he was. "How could we ask you to suffer for us if we hadn't suffered to find you? I gave my freedom, knowing you'd help me and I'd help you. I gave you my trust long before we had even met, hoping you'd do the same."

"That was a pretty big gamble."

"I gambled everything. We all did. But here you are, and here I am—and we're both free."

"Thanks for not eating me in the dungeon." I smiled. "I honestly didn't think I'd make it out of there alive, anyway. I thought I might as well try to free as many as I could before they killed me."

Zephyr laughed. "I doubt very much that Solas would have allowed you to die at anyone's hands. If you think you suffered, imagine if he wasn't there to keep the worst of it from your room."

"I didn't peg him for a softy, Zeph," I answered back.

"No one calls me *Zeph*." He jerked his full attention to me, his brow pulled tight.

"If you're not going to stop calling me a Crow, I'll call you whatever I want."

Solas landed beside me, driving his fist into the ground from the force of the fall. The air thinned and cooled. "A softie I'm not, but paying my debts for your safety would have been pointless if I'd have let you die in the end."

"I'm glad to know you're clearing up your debts." Disappointment filled me. "Don't do me any favors, Solas."

"Eat it," Zephyr growled at me, and I knew what he meant. I swallowed my magick.

I let Zephyr wrap me in shadows and bring me to the door to my bedroom, leaving Solas in the forest. His parting words were for my ears alone, to hide how powerful my Malice was. Hanging a witch in Elphame was not unheard of, and one of my power would find a rope around their neck mighty fast. Did I think Solas would be the one to tie the noose? No. But there were eyes and ears in every nook and cranny of Elphame.

Zephyr said he would talk to Solas about bringing me to see Solas' grandmother, Elda. She saw all but spoke to few. If anyone knew what I must do next, it would be her, if she'd even talk to me. I was willing to chance it if it brought me closer to going home, away from this place, away from Solas and Faolan and every other bloody Fae, save Nix and my creature.

"The hate you feel for Solas is misplaced," Zephyr said before he walked off. "He did it to save you, to keep you alive—just as you had become a monster to save others."

"It worked."

He shook his head. "No, little Crow, I think you're angry because you don't hate him, because you think you should, because you want a target for your anger. He's a better man than I am."

"Why do you say that?"

"Because he'll take it until the day you die, all your hate and blame and anger. He'll take it all to ease your pain. I won't." He turned on his heel. "Prepare for tonight. Elda always says yes to Solas. To the Sluagh caves we'll go, for answers that'll hurt even more than ignorance."

"I'd expect nothing less from this place," I replied.

Tonight was somewhere between a fool's errand and risking my life, which pretty much summed up my time, to date, in Elphame. If anything, I was getting better at making choices when stuck between impossibilities.

Chapter Seven

Elda, Claviger of Dreams, Master of Mirrors, the grandmother of Solas, lived in the caves of the Sluagh. Chains of long narrow tunnels, which linked the great lunar caverns, could not be seen with the naked eye. The entrance, tucked behind layers of shadows and magick, carved by teeth and claws, felt wrong. Just standing near the opening sent my mind into a panic, warnings fired from the most ancient places within my brain.

Run.

Hide.

Turn back.

From the rock ledge, I watched as the black clouds rolled with life. Creatures from above landed on the rocks and clutched the stones—waiting, watching. They were nothing short of terrifying and even less to celebrate. Zephyr had tucked me into his shadows and dropped me on the windy ledge of the Sluagh but went no further. This was not a group task, and he couldn't enter unless invited. He was not Sluagh and would not be coming. I stood on the ledge and thought, for the briefest of moments, that I could jump and end it all.

"You'd survive the fall if you pushed out far enough from the ledge," Solas said as his feet landed beside me from above. "I have my doubts on the landing, though. There's nothing but dagger-sharp stones and bones at the bottom."

"Landings always hurt more than the fall." I leaned over the edge and smiled. We'd had a similar conversation the day I'd come to Elphame.

Jagged rocks and trees painted the side of the cliff. I pulled back as the wind rolled up the side and tried desperately to pull me off. Out from the ledge, it felt like I could see all Elphame. But no amount of trying would let me see home from here. I wondered if I ever would see it again.

"They're not watching *you*, are they?" I asked as I scanned the skies and rocky sides. Eyes glinted in the moonlight.

"No. But I belong here. You don't."

"Are you like them? Can you change into one of them?" I asked.

"No, I can't change into one of them. But, in a sense, we are the same. We come from the same place, from similar lines. I can call the magick of the Sluagh, the darkness, and can look pretty scary to those who don't know, but it's nothing more than smoke and mirrors. I am as I appear. What lies below the skin, though, is a much darker story. I don't think your mortal mind would handle seeing all I can be."

"We're all monsters under the skin," I answered and fought the urge to squirm. "Now that I'm here, I'd rather not be."

"Then we leave." Solas waited for me to decide. "We can leave—no harm, no foul. You're not being forced to be here, Perdi. This was for you, for answers you wanted."

"If I leave, I'll kick myself later," I answered and turned to the mouth of the cave.

Solas stepped to the side and extended his arm. "Go ahead."

"Alone?" I stammered.

"Do you need me to hold your hand?" he asked and grinned. "I thought you'd prefer me out here, blocking the entrance. You don't want to be in there when they decide to come in after you. You are the first mortal to enter these caves."

"No. Good point. Stay out here." I finally answered and turned to the mouth of the rocky cave. Before I could take a step, I looked back at him. "Don't leave me here, please."

"I've never left you, Perdi, not once. I've always been close by." Solas grabbed my hand and squeezed. "I'd bring down every cliff to find you."

I believed him, and I stepped into the gaping hole. I couldn't shake the feeling I had walked through the gates of hell, the Gate to Elphame, all over again. I stopped, not twenty feet in, and held onto the wall. I couldn't get enough air. My chest tightened. The surrounding stone pushed down on me like an invisible force, crushing the life from my bones, wringing the light from my soul. I was in another stone prison. It smelled of the caves in the basement of the Golden Court. Along the wall, I felt small scrapings made into the stone and thought of the nail marks in my cell. I tried to scream, but fear had frozen me in place.

"You're not trapped," Solas spoke behind me. "You're free."

I nodded. My mouth was too bone dry to agree out loud.

"I swear on all that is mine to give, you are safe, you are free and you can leave whenever you want. No one here will force you to do anything you don't want to do, and even then, they'll double-check with me to make sure."

I turned back once more. "Just don't go, please. No matter what. Promise me, Solas."

"I promise. I will stay right here. Zephyr is at the bottom, waiting. We've got you, and we won't leave you here."

I closed my eyes and shook my head until I drowned out the thoughts of my Taking and spending my first nights in the Golden Court dungeon. I told myself Solas wouldn't bring me to this place only to be eaten and tortured. He wouldn't bring me here if it were just another prison. I had to trust he wouldn't leave me here, but the nagging thought in the back of my mind told me that trusting another Fae for a second time was stupider than the first. Because now I knew better. I had already suffered once for it. But Solas, however conniving he was, was also practical. He wouldn't have wasted his time by bringing me to this place. I told myself that Nix and Orrian would have warned me.

I opened my eyes, calm, centered and in control. Once the panic was gone and my vision cleared, the tunnel wasn't as terrifying as I'd thought at first. The walls were littered with tiny crystals, like little stars. The darkness felt like an eternity, made of the night sky. It was like opening my eyes inside of the shadows, calm darkness. I moved along the side of the cave. The stone was smooth, rubbed flat by hundreds of years of use. It felt like hours to move from the mouth to the womb of the cave, the end. The tunnel opened into a massive black chamber. Little torches mounted on the wall chased away the dark. The room was bare, save for the center. In the middle of the room, on a dais of stone, sat a small woman on pillows.

"Elda?" I called out, my eyes roaming the room. The woman lifted her head and motioned me forward. "Pardon me. I'm looking for Elda."

"And so, you've found her," the woman replied.

I froze and looked behind then above. "I'm sorry, but where is she?"

"In front of you, child. Were you expecting a beast?" She smiled. "Sit, dear Finis."

"Finis?" I cocked my head to the side. "My name is Perdi."

"And so, it is. Finis is nothing more than a term of endearment for your kind. Now sit and speak of why you've come."

"But, you're human." I pointed out the obvious. "How can you be Solas' grandmother?"

"Once you get to my age, you are grandmother to all." She smiled and motioned for me to sit with her. "Once, so long ago I don't remember, I was like you, half in this world and half in the mortal. My father was of the Sluagh line. My mother was human. When I came to Elphame, I stayed far too long. The longer I remained in Elphame, the more of Elphame I became. After those many years, I couldn't return. I was no longer human. I'd be cut off from Fae, from the force of who I had become."

"Did you ever want to leave?" I asked.

She nodded. "Several times, I have wished for the mortal realm. But many had left before me and had gone mad from grief, cut off from their very balance."

"Crows?" I asked, and she nodded.

"They had become Elphame, and upon their return, they were neither Fae nor human. That is enough for madness."

I raised my brows. "We always thought it was what happened to them here that caused their madness."

"For some, they were not mad. They were simply broken with no means to repair the damage." She kept her eyes on me, and I fought not to look away from her gaze. "I see you wonder the same about yourself…if you are too broken, well beyond repair."

I nodded but didn't trust my voice.

"Only you have the answer to that question, my child. There is nothing that can't be fixed, but the work required, at times, can be harder than living with the pain." She reached for my face, and I flinched at first but let her hold my jaw in her small, warm hands. Into my eyes she looked then pulled away with a smile. "I see why Zephyr is so protective of you. He always has been, even before you stepped through the Gate. He spoke of you as if you and he had been friends for many lifetimes. He's been preparing for your arrival for just as long. You and he battle the same wars inside your souls."

"If he hadn't eaten my pearl, he wouldn't feel it," I countered.

"It is not your pearl that troubles him. If anything, it offers him calm. You are linked, bound together, you and he, and he will finally find his peace through you—a calmness he so deserves."

"I seriously doubt that. I don't have a calm bone in my body. I've got war and death in my bones," I replied. My voice wasn't as brave as I wanted it to be. "I don't want to be linked to him. I just want to go home. I know everyone has all these plans for me and brought me here for a reason, but I just want to go home."

"We all seek a home."

I smiled weakly. "My dad… Do you know what happened to him?"

Elda closed her eyes and nodded. "I'm sorry, my child. I do not see him."

I scrunched my face and fought not to break down. "How? Is he dead?"

"I stopped seeing him the moment of your Taking."

My heart was absolutely smashed, and all my hope had leaked out with her news, news I had already known. I hung my head. I feared this moment, learning of his death, but deep down, I knew it before I had stepped foot in Elphame. Everything always circled back to Faolan. Even if he didn't land the killing blow upon my father, he was who I blamed. "I want to go home."

"Do you know what kept your greatest grandmother on these lands?" She pulled me to the surface of my drowning grief.

"No," I answered solemnly. "We had suspected she had died as long ago as she had been born. It wasn't until the Fae came to my home for my Taking that I discovered she had even lived."

"It was your line which caused the opening, the very Gate that took countless lives. Three Darkmore witches heard the faint call of Elphame. They caused a Gate between the fabric of Elphame and humanity. Not realizing what they had done, it was your line who bedded a Fae and created the first halfling. Not long after, the horror of Elphame set in. And when they tried to stop it, it was too late. Fae had tasted mankind. The worse of Elphame became a reality for the mortal world. Fae took who they pleased, killed thousands upon thousands. In return, thousands of Fae had fallen at the hands of humans. A war brewed between us both.

"To save us all, three Darkmore witches and the Kings of Elphame signed oaths. And through the years, the Fae tracked the Darkmore line, slaughtering all but one, Aoife, who was placed under the protection of Solas." Elda poured tea for us both. She reminded me of every grandmother I had met—soft, yet terrifying if you cornered one of their grandchildren. "As your line opened the Gate, only your line can close it. Aoife came here knowing she'd never return. She came here and cursed her line, cursed all Elphame. She cursed you, Perdita, in hopes you'd come and fight to close the Gate your very blood helped open."

"I read about her sacrifice, her last entry, in the journals."

"Solas helped her get here. He sacrificed his own people to get her across. We were forbidden never to bring a Darkmore to these lands again, but Solas disobeyed and made the ultimate sacrifice—everything he's ever loved, his home, his people, his soul. When he brought you, he did it once again. He was tasked with killing you at the Gate, should you be too powerful. The Golden King wanted you, but not if you were too powerful to control. And when you crossed over, Solas felt all of who you are. The very grounds of Elphame shuddered when you set foot here, and even I, in these caves, felt you cross. But he did not kill you. He lied and let you live. All on a whimper of hope did he give everything to ensure your survival."

"I didn't know that part."

"We all gave our freedoms and lives willingly if it meant this would end."

"Why would you give your freedom or your life for a human? We're the only ones who suffer."

"Silly girl, only the soulless would willingly partake in the torture of children. I've seen hundreds of children marched through our lands to pay a price they didn't deserve. Their screams echoed throughout all Elphame. There was not a place you could hide from the savageness of what has been done and what will be done."

"Why would they want another Darkmore? If it's forbidden to take us, why not just kill me when I got here, end the threat we pose and the Darkmore line completely?"

"That is the question, isn't it? They thought they could win you. If they couldn't, some did plan to kill you in the end, but not before they got their final tithe from your line—a child."

I shuddered. "I never thought it would be Faolan who would do this to me. I trusted him."

"To protect your people, could you not turn on him? Could you not kill him?"

I nodded. "To protect innocent people, yes. But killing me was never about keeping his people safe. He did it for greed, for power, for control."

"I did not say he would kill you, merely some would see you dead. What his intentions were, I cannot say." She corrected me. Semantics was all that was. Just because it wouldn't be him that landed the killing blow doesn't mean he wouldn't be to blame. "What do you think would have happened to his people had he said no, had he protected you as you needed?"

"That doesn't make it right," I countered.

"True, but it doesn't make it wrong, either. You know as well as anyone the things we must do, who we must become, to survive. The balance of it all, doing what is needed over what's wanted, doing what is right for the many over the one and saving as many as you can in the process. Selecting those to sacrifice for the lives of their people is the burden of every king."

I scowled at her response. I hadn't come for the reminder of the monster still lurking in the shadows of my soul.

"I did not say I agree or disagree with who Faolan became or who he will grow to become. I am telling you I understand the need to protect your people at all costs, and for some, the cost is their soul."

"Rape and torture… No one must become that big a monster," I countered.

"Be thankful you've never been faced with that choice."

"Why are you defending those monsters?" I asked, my temper flaring. I swore the temperature rose with the boil of my anger.

"You have come here for answers. No one said you would like the answers you'd receive, child. I am not defending anyone for their actions, but I also will not judge them by choices I've not had to make myself. You cannot plunge a man into atrocities and expect him not to adapt. After thousands of years of war, death and destruction, Elphame is what remains and what will continue to remain. You either adjust your moral compass or you die. The world, mortal and Fae, demands that only the strongest can survive."

"Adapt..." I whispered, and I shuddered at the thought of my own adjustments made to survive.

She nodded. "Indeed, it is a bleak future when we build thrones of blood and bones."

"Where do I fit into this future of Elphame?" I asked.

"Not just you and not just Elphame. We all have stakes in this outcome, Perdita. For, as many who will live, will die. If the Gate remains open, people will die on both sides, as it has always been. If the Gate closes and there are no Crows to take outside of Elphame, the inner wars will begin once again. The only time there has been any peace across these lands has been at the cost of your realm, at the cost of the lesser Fae."

"What do I do?" I asked.

"You do nothing and watch your fate become that of another mortal, or you can finish what Aoife started and close the Gate for good."

"And what cost shall I bear for this?" I asked.

"Wise girl. There is always a cost, isn't there?" She smiled softly. "The cost is your human life."

"It'll kill me?" I was surprised.

"All magick, especially Malice, has a price for use, Perdita. You know this. You know the rule of thrice. Three Darkmore witches have already given their lives to this spell—Aoife, your mother, who knew you'd be Taken, and you are the third. You will be the one who pays the highest price." Each word was another rock placed on my grave. "I see two outcomes for you, Perdita. I've dreamed of both. One, you are found dead, bloodied and bruised, puffy from a long pain. But faintly, I also see you trapped here in Elphame for good. I do not know which end will result in closing the

Gate. But I do see war. No matter your choice, I see war coming and a fearsome battle."

"What happens after the Gate is closed?"

"Fae caught in the human world will be cut off from Elphame and the magick that makes them Fae. They would likely perish if they could not return. Humans still in the Fae world would be trapped for all time. Battles will be fought and won. Death will come and go. But balance will be found."

"My choices are a painful death and being stranded in Elphame. It doesn't really sound like there are many options to choose from."

"Does it matter? In the end, does the fate of one halfling matter when the rest of our worlds are on the brink of war?" she asked in return. "Would you churn the choices over and over, weighing the options best suited for only you?

"No," I answered truthfully. "I suppose not."

"This is your sacrifice to bear and yours alone. The choices are yours to make, and I envy you none of them."

I nodded and finished my tea in silence. I would die, or I would never go home. Both were painful truths that were hard to wash down with my spiced tea. Grief washed over me, as it often did at random times, replacing my carefully constructed lie of normality. I closed my eyes and let it come. To fight it was useless. I let it settle in my bones, where it wouldn't budge. Layers upon layers, I'd have to rip back and stare into the painful truth of my existence, both healing and terrifying at once.

"The pain you feel, the questioning and blame, you're not alone in this," she added as I stood. She touched my hand for the briefest of moments and pulled back, rubbing her knuckles. "I had to know."

"Know what?" I asked.

She smiled. "If you were the one."

"To close the Gate?"

"No, the one Solas was meant to save. The Crow who would love him. I needed to know if the favors he sold were worth the cost."

"I didn't know he sold favors." I frowned. I let the other part fall to the side. But I knew I had only wanted to hate him and never could. "He never mentioned it. What did it cost him?"

"How could he tell you? He juggled both heaven and hell. And your hate for him was once as pure as glacier water. As to the costs, those are his to share." Her answer left me with more questions. "The day you sold a piece of yourself to Zephyr, the Sluagh were coming for you."

"I thought they were coming to kill me," I answered.

"Any other day, they would have—not out of hate, but out of sorrow, out of pity for you. We felt your pain, heard your cries, tasted your tears in the wind and rain. We heard you beg for help, for death. We did what we could to keep you safe as you ran. The Sluagh must carefully balance which wars we will start and finish. But Solas? He came to save you and spared no cost." Her eyes glittered like the night, tears glistening on her cheeks. "You are not alone in your pain. We share in it, for we're all looking over the same abyss and wondering if we will be pushed or will jump willingly."

"Don't you see all?"

"It is both a burden and a curse to have the sight. But not even I can see what choices you'll make—only the possible outcomes," she answered with a sigh. "I do not see my end. I do not see the end for those I love. I merely glimpse the possibilities of those tied to it."

"Thank you for meeting with me," I said as I stepped down from her dais.

"I would wish you long life, but I'm not sure if that's what you're hoping for, so I will wish you a painless end."

"I wish… I wish for you to have one night where your dreams are everything you want in life and nothing like what I know you dream."

She smiled. "That, dear Perdi, is one of the nicest wishes I've been given."

I left her where I found her, alone in her cave. The farther I moved away from her, the less I left the numbness. It was replaced with everything at once. The frozen fear that kept me from feeling anything at all was gone. I was given the truth without needing to barter for it. I was given brutal honesty that burned me to my core, but it was my truth, and I didn't have to trade a chunk of my soul for it, although it felt like I'd left my soul on the ground at her feet, trampled on and beyond any repair.

At the mouth of the cave, Solas stood. He didn't leave me. I ran from the tunnels, and for the briefest of moments, I could fly. I heard the start of Solas' scream, but the darkness wrapped around me and pulled me from the plummet. I almost regretted being caught.

"Zephyr," I whispered into the shadows gripped tightly around me.

"Yes?"

"I'm going to die here, in Elphame," I finally said.

"I know."

"It's going to hurt."

"Everything hurts in Elphame. Make it count."

The shadows left me in my room, alone in my thoughts, alone with my sadness and anger and my need to seek vengeance against Faolan, against everyone who brought me to this godforsaken place. Even in freedom, I wasn't truly free. My choices were few, and neither brought me closer to home. I dropped to my knees. The weight of Elphame crushed me. It squeezed out everything good until I was nothing but pain. It took everything from me—everything worth having, worth loving. It took my father, and now I was utterly alone in the world, both in the mortal realm and Elphame.

The rage flowed from the pit of fire in my stomach and didn't stop. I didn't want it to stop. It tore out of me in a burning cry. It kept coming even after my voice was gone and my tears had dried. The room exploded into bits of wood and glass from the force expelled from my soul. Numb, I curled into a ball and watched as the walls licked with the flames of my pain. I wanted it all to burn, from the Dark Courts to the highest peaks in Elphame. I'd bathe in the ashes of this godforsaken place. I'd choke them all for each Crow Taken.

"Perdi," Solas called from the threshold of the room, but I didn't answer. "I'm right here. I've always been right here."

I watched him move through the wind and fire of my grief. The flames crawled over his flesh, but he didn't burn. He held out his hand and pushed through the wreckage, reaching for me. Chunks of falling embers landed and burned away clothes, leaving not a mark on his skin. The moment the flames touched him, they vanished in a wisp of smoke, gone under the cool breeze that flowed from his soul. He could claim the fires in hell as his own.

"You're not alone. You've never been alone." His voice cut through the storm like thunder. He crawled to my side and grabbed my hand. The moment he touched me, the storm stopped, debris fell and the flames extinguished. His touch was cold against the burn within me. His very touch stopped my world from spinning out of control. I fought the urge to pull away and let it all burn around us. The satisfaction I'd feel, I was willing to bet, would be worth it.

"My dad is gone," I cried out. "I'm the only one left, Solas. I have no one left who loves me. No one left who will protect me. I'm alone."

"That's not true."

I shook my head. "No, there's no one who will protect me simply because I'm worth protecting. Here, in Elphame, I'm nothing more than a pawn—a tool to be used up until I die. No one wants me to live because my life has value."

Solas pulled me into his chest and wrapped himself around me until all I could smell was him. "I will protect you, Perdi, for no other reason than because you are worthy of protection and love and kindness."

I pulled my head back. I needed him to see the look on his face. I needed him to know I couldn't be anything more than who and what I am. "We both know I'm only here because you want me to close the Gate."

"That's not true. I protected you even when I didn't think you were the one to close the Gate, and I will keep protecting you whether you do it or not."

"What would happen to your people if I left or didn't close it?"

Solas hugged her tighter. "You don't need to worry about my people. I have protected them for this long, and I will keep protecting them long after you."

"What about *my* people?" I asked.

He sighed. "I want to lie, to make this feel less horrible. The truth is, the Taking will continue until the Gate is closed or until all Elphame decides against it. The Gate will rot long before Elphame chooses not to Take Crows.

"Am I a debt you must pay?" I lifted my face to his. I looked into his eyes to see his truth.

"No, that's not what I meant."

"Then what did you mean?"

"Many oaths were made to get you here. Many innocent people put their lives on the line to get you to my door. I paid those debts willingly to ensure your safety. But you weren't just a debt. It was a poor choice of words. You are someone worth sacrifice, worth any cost I can pay freely."

"What did it cost you?" I asked.

He shook his head. "There are some things better left unsaid."

"What did it cost you, Solas?" I demanded. "How do you expect me to trust you when you keep me from the truth?"

"Some truths are harder to say out loud than others. For some, I paid in gems and jewels—worthless trinkets I care nothing for, to keep you from their advances at court. For others, I helped with land and homes. Many of the oaths made to the Lesser Fae and the wee folk, I paid in seeds and herbs, moving trees, repairing roofs," he answered, then closed his eyes. "But there were those I dealt with who are much more brutal than I could ever become. The price for those deals was me. It cost nights with me. It cost me pain and relearning what hurt feels like. To others, I am the darkness that lurks in the shadows, and I paid for their fear with my own."

"Why would you do that? I'm just a Crow." My last words came out strangled.

He lifted my chin and dabbed away my tears. "You're more than that. You're my fate."

"Your fate?"

"From the day I was born, I have lived for this very moment. My grandmother spoke of the day I would give my kingdom for a Crow. I'd offer my life for someone in the here and the there…a halfling. I've dreamed of you, and I've waited. It is how Zephyr and I became close, a shared destiny with the Crow. Like his, my fate is tied to yours and always has been. I have prepared for you from the day I was born. Decades after decades came and went with a new Crow during every Tithe. And each time, I tried to save them and failed. When Zephyr gave himself, I thought he was a fool. I didn't think the Gods would ever allow you to come. I thought it was a cruel joke of Fate to have given me so much hope and never bring you.

"When finally, I saw you, I knew you were the very one my grandmother spoke of—the one Zephyr had spoken of. I felt it in my blood when your magick first touched me. I felt it when you took power from the Gate. I fought to hide the truth from you, and each time I tried to show you I wasn't like the rest, I changed my mind. I couldn't risk countless lives in hopes you would believe me. I couldn't risk you or what suffering you'd endure for my kindness. Your hate for me was so pure. I could hold it in my hands."

"I feared you more than any other in these lands. I wish I would have known."

"I do not recall you fearing me a single time—not when we got to Elphame, certainly not when you stabbed me twice, nor when I found you again. You were brave and still are. You have been the only one ever to meet my eyes."

"How else do you talk to someone?" I huffed a small laugh.

"But that's the very thing… You see me as *someone* and not just a monster. It was pleasantly surprising and scary at the same time."

"You did not fear me," I countered.

"Every single day. Not because I felt you become a monster, but because you calmed the one inside me."

"I think I feared who I was when you were near. I fought so hard to become someone to be afraid of, but near you, that mask kept slipping. I was scared of what would happen if I showed you who I really was, that maybe you wouldn't like that part of me, either. Scared you would try to stop me," I answered. "I saw what you did, all the times you tried to keep me safe from myself. You purposely became my target and took so much of my hate and anger."

"I did it to keep you alive. I saw the real you, even when you didn't want me to. And it killed me to still make the decisions I had to make. The choices I made were for the protection of those who were worse off than you. As much as I wanted to save you, I wouldn't sentence them to death for you."

"I'd never ask that of anyone."

"And now you're here, and I don't know how to save you. I don't know how to make you want to live. I'm terrified every minute of every day that I won't save you, that I'll wake up and you'll be gone—that I'm not monster enough to protect you, and I'll lose you. I can't lose you, Perdi...not now, not ever."

His words felt like a warm fire on a winter's night. He didn't know of my fate, only his own. I opened my mouth to tell him what Elda had said but said nothing. My fate was my own, a road I must walk alone. I smiled and let go of the grief strangling me. I cupped his face and kissed him. "Thank you for wanting to save me, for always being just around the corner, ready to pluck a Crow out of a net."

"Thank you for wanting to save *me*. I knew you would." Solas echoed my words into my mouth as he leaned down and kissed me back. "Your first night here, you promised me that you'd save me, too, and I believed you. And when you were leaving, you came back for me. You were finally free, but you reached through the darkness for me. You're the first who has ever come back for me."

"You never left me," I whispered. "Not once."

"Never."

His movements were nothing like I expected them to be. He was soft, almost hesitant, scared to move too suddenly and scare me away. He held my face and brushed his lips against mine delicately. But I wasn't breakable, not any longer. I didn't want calm. I needed the chaos that was the man in my arms. I didn't need to be coddled, and I certainly didn't enjoy the sympathy I felt with his movements. I dug my hands into his hair, tugging him closer as I opened my mouth to his.

Solas groaned. A hint of growl vibrated down my throat and into my stomach, sending heat coursing through me, burning away the frost still resting in my core. I breathed him in as deeply as I could and let it melt away my fear and distrust and pain. Let it raze through me, wave after wave of darkness that was Solas. Another growl gripped my core and cleansed the blood from my hands, the memory of what I had to do to get here, to gain my freedom. I gave myself to his calm fire, to him, as he roamed my body with his hands, unbuttoning and unclothing me as he went.

He pulled back, breathless, and picked me off the floor. With my legs around his waist, he carried me to a destroyed bed. He crawled across it on all fours, throwing shards of wood and art to the floor as I greedily ate from his mouth. Our ragged and hungry breathing was the only sound left in the room. As softly as he had removed my clothes, I ripped his from his body in jerks and tears. His shirt, tattered and unrepairable, landed on the floor. I pushed myself into his naked chest and yanked on his belt, jerking and tugging until his pants were next to be thrown from the bed.

Solas eased onto me. The heat from both of us left us slick with need. And when I couldn't get enough, he held me closer until not a part of my body wasn't covered by his. The hunger twisting inside of my belly softened with his touch. He whispered my name and kissed my neck and shoulders, turned my back to his chest and touched the parts of me I tried to hide. He danced his fingers along my side as he dragged his tongue down my back, over the scars from a lashing I would never forget. And when I pulled away to hide, he held me tighter.

"I'll see them dead before they touch you again." Solas whispered his promises into the marks left behind by Elphame.

He kissed every inch of my back. A kiss for every mark. A kiss for every wound I endured and one more for every fear it left me with. My body relaxed. I believed him. I trusted him. I turned to face him and gently, finally calmed, kissed him as though I had spent decades kissing him before and had known his body for just as long.

I watched his face as I touched his body, slowly, softly, as though he were the one to break. His flesh was unmarred, a perfect alabaster as if the Gods themselves had carved him. But I knew not all scars could be seen, and some of the worst were buried deep inside. Emotional pain leaves invisible scars, yet with the gentlest of touches, it can be traced by those who care enough to feel for them.

"I'll see them dead before they touch you again." I whispered my own promises into his mouth. "I swear to the Gods."

"Of that, I have no doubt," Solas breathed into my neck.

When it was over and I was jelly, he crawled back up my body and covered me with the remnants of my bedding.

"What about you?" I murmured with loose and soggy words.

"That, Perdi, was for me and exactly what I've always wanted to do." He pulled me tight against his body and breathed in my scent. "If ever I am given this pleasure again, it can't be on a mattress on the floor."

"I'm sorry about the room." My laugh came out as a yawn, and I pushed myself into Solas as far as I could. I was safe.

"It doesn't matter. It's only a bedroom." He kissed my forehead. "Sleep. I'll be right here."

"Don't leave me," I whispered and pulled his warmth around me, tucked in the safety of the darkness that was Solas. There was no safer place than in the arms of the very nightmares that haunted Elphame.

As I slowly drifted, Solas whispered to me, letting me know he wouldn't leave. I wasn't alone. My heart broke a little more when he murmured my name. I was his destiny, and his fate was to pick my dead body off the ground. I'd die here and kill whatever good was left inside of him. To finally find love, the kind that pierced your very soul, only to know I'd leave it behind? That was a special kind of pain, the kind only Gods laughed about.

Chapter Eight

The morning came wrapped in shadows. The night had given me peace for once. I hadn't dreamed of death at my hands. There were no screams of terror or pleas for mercy to rattle my dreams and leave my throat raw. I had slept deeply, with Solas at my side and shadows dancing in the corner. He had stayed through the night and into the morning, waking me before he left to deal with court business. Once he left, the shadows covered me.

"You're never that far away." I rolled onto my back and stared up into the nothingness that surrounded me. At times, I'd see the night. Other times, it was a void of various shades of black, always moving against themselves.

"No, we're not."

"Are you Zephyr, or are you shadows?" I asked.

"Shadows. You'll learn to tell us apart. He comes as a force, with a wind that burns or freezes, depending on why he's coming. We come as night. You never really notice us until you're already in the dark."

"I don't feel that when Zephyr is around," I answered. "He feels familiar, like home."

"You are bound to him. He'll always feel that way to you. But trust us when we say, to others, he feels like death pushing against the front door… Frozen terror."

"If he's at their front door, they deserve why he's not bothering to knock." I sighed at who I knew he was, deep inside. He was hell and fire and dread, but he was my friend for better or worse. I breathed in the smell of rain and forest. "Why do you cry?"

"We do not cry."

"You smell like tears," I answered. "And you feel like sadness."

"We smell of you," they answered.

"I'm not sad."

"You will be." They moved tighter around me.

"Why?"

"The court business Solas left for. It is about you. It will hurt you."

"Doesn't it always?" I sighed.

"Do not let him hide you away or shelter you. You deserve the truth. Anything less is just another prison in Elphame," they said, and I grinned just a little to know they had been spying and bringing me back information.

"Does Zephyr know you spy on everyone?" I asked.

"Not always," they answered. "But for you, we share willingly."

"Has Solas been lying to me?" I asked. My heart palpitated.

"So far, not that we know of. Today, however, there was an omission of truth. Keeping you from the truth, that is a lie wrapped up to look pretty. But those are the lies that hurt the most," they answered. "Do not allow him to keep your truths away from you. We live and die over less in Elphame."

Before I could ask more questions, the shadows pulled from me. Zephyr always called them back. He never let them stay away for too long. I wondered how often they spied for him as they did for me. And did Zephyr hear what they said to me? He didn't mention it, but I also didn't hear anything I shouldn't have known. I dressed and made my way through the halls of the Dark Court, my mind on Solas and the potential new prison I now lived in. With each step, the walls grew narrower, tight against my shoulders. I stopped at the foot of the stairs and calmed myself. I closed my eyes and breathed until the feeling of being trapped had finally flowed from my knotted gut.

Whatever conversation Zephyr and Solas had been having stopped the moment I stepped into the room for breakfast. Zephyr grinned like a prepubescent boy, and Solas smiled. It was a smile I could feel in my soul. I felt a little less crazed when I woke in the arms of Solas, like the gashes within my soul had begun to scab over.

Zephyr pushed out a chair with his foot at the head of the table for me. It screeched across the floor and came to an abrupt stop at my side. "Little Crow."

"Always the gentleman, Zeph." I shook my head. He grinned at both the nickname and my joke. "It's a wonder why you're not crawling with ladies."

"I'm saving myself." Zephyr winked and smiled knowingly. "How was your night? Get any sleep?"

I filled my plate and took a seat at the opposite end of the table from Solas. "I slept great, and you, Solas?"

"Once I put out a small fire, I slept like a rock, thank you," he answered and stared at me through his lashes. The grin on his face was unmistakable. Something inside him had changed as much as it had changed me.

"Me? Well, thank you for asking," Zephyr blurted. "I would have slept better if it weren't for Solas' name echoing up and down the hall for hours."

I blushed. "Huh, weird. I didn't hear a thing. I must have slept right through it."

"That's what all the girls say." Zephyr laughed, and I couldn't help but join him.

"Thanks, Perdi." Solas shook his head. "Nix wanted me to let you know he would be joining Elswyth on her journey. He'll return in a few days."

I nodded. "They're pretty close, her and Nix."

"They were very much like you and him. Before he went to the mortal world, Nix promised her he'd find her again..." Zephyr paused and looked at my confused face. "What? I pay attention to court gossip, just like everyone else does. How else do you expect me to always have answers?"

My grin widened. "Sorry, continue."

"What I'm saying is, he saw her as his sister and promised to find her again. It would be his duty, as her kin, to accompany her to her new home. Nix takes his duty seriously. It truly is life and death for him."

I nodded. "I'm glad he found her again."

Zephyr let the weight of his judgmental stare rest on my shoulders until I shivered. "You need to fix things with your gnome before it kills him."

"She doesn't need to do a damn thing," Solas interjected.

"Like hell, she doesn't." Zephyr shook his head at him and turned back to me. "Yes. You do. He gave everything to you and for you. He went into the cursed mortal world for you, cut off from everything he knew and loved. He did that for you. And today, Nix left the only home he has left because he was scared that he was offending you with his presence. He only left because you wouldn't stop rotting in your bedroom like a piece of meat in the sun. He sees you as the only family he has left, and he went away out of respect for your feelings. Time and time again, he's willingly fought by your side and at risk of his very life. That's bullshit, Perdi. You owe him more than that, more than this abuse. You may be able to get away with this shit with Solas, but I'll call you on it every time."

"Stop, Zephyr," Solas warned him. A trickle of darkness seeped into the air around him like the sun had instantly set, leaving only the night behind.

"Oh, please. Your temper doesn't scare me in the least. Pull your darkness back in before this conversation is better had outside, away from the breakables." Zephyr turned from Solas, ignoring the warning and placing his full attention back on me. "You've spent days, little Crow, crying that you're all alone, that no one loves you, that no one cares. Yet, you never once stopped to think that Nix is all alone, that he has only your love left in his entire world. He cares so deeply for you that he left. Now, he's as alone as you felt. You're a selfish woman who doesn't deserve his loyalty or his life. I, for one, would kill for that loyalty, that love, that unflinching willingness to die for me and not have it because of oaths or courts or gains. Simply because I was loved that deeply."

I opened my mouth to say I owed no one, but Zephyr was right. Instead, I nodded. "You're right."

"I know I'm right, little Crow. You have friends here. Don't screw them up with your sadness and grief that they didn't cause. They've been through enough. They don't need to go through the hell that is Perdita. Now that I've said my piece, you do with it what you want." Zephyr stood. "I'll catch up with you later, Solas."

"Wait! Did I interrupt something?" I asked.

Zephyr shook his head. "Not at all. This is your home, not mine. Court business can wait."

I frowned. "What did I interrupt?" And when he didn't spit it out, I looked to Solas. "Now is not the time to start keeping secrets, Solas. Secrets damn near killed me once. I'm not doing it again. You want me to trust you, but how can I when you're not truthful? When you keep things from me?"

"I'm not keeping things from you. I'm trying to protect you."

Zephyr cleared his throat and glanced at Solas. "I told you she wouldn't like being kept out of the loop. But do you ever listen to me?"

"This is withholding, not protection," I countered. "This isn't the path I will walk down with you. You're either straight with me or point me in the direction of Nix. I'll take my chances out there with him, where I'll suffer, but at least I'll always know where I stand. It's your choice. You can choose if you want to walk my path with me or be left behind. But you better remember when I gave you a chance and you screwed it all up. There will only ever be one chance, one warning."

"You sound like Zephyr." Solas threw his hands in the air and groaned. "But, you're right. Obviously, I'm not going about it the right way. I'm sorry. I'm trying and failing. I thought, truly, that not involving you would be a respite you'd appreciate, that you wouldn't want to be involved."

"When I said I wanted protection, I meant protecting me from physical harm. When someone takes a swing at me, stop them. That's protection. But you can't protect my heart." I spoke softly. "Solas, I don't need a babysitter. I need someone at my side who will face the horror with me, not shove me in a box, hidden from the truth. I'll decide if I want to be involved, not you."

Solas frowned but eventually nodded to Zephyr.

Zephyr sat back down and pulled out a small envelope. "Two problems on our plate for today. What would you like first, the bad news or the worse news?"

"Bad news first," I answered.

"The gargoyles have awoken," Solas answered.

"I didn't know they were all asleep, but yes, there's one in my bedroom. Seth is his name," I answered. Both Solas and Zephyr groaned. "I asked you before what the significance of them was. We didn't really discuss it."

Solas groaned again, pained. He pointed to Zephyr to fill me in. "Zephyr knows more about the gargoyles than I do. Zephyr is war, and so are they, whereas I'm just death."

"Gargoyles only wake during times of war and no other time. Once, long ago, they were Mares and helped only the Royals. But those days are too long ago to remember why they stopped. The fact you have one in your bedroom tells us war is coming, that he's given you his name says the war is coming for you." Zephyr spoke plainly, not sugar coating anything. I liked that most about him.

"Well then, I'm scared to ask what the worse news is now. I mean, what could be worse than war?" I responded then flinched at memories I wanted to push back down.

Zephyr slid the envelope to me and patted my hand. He felt me cringe when I touched the letter. The envelope had Solas' name printed on the front in scriptwriting. "Faolan… He's invited Solas to a meeting in the Court of Less. He wants to discuss a peace treaty."

"He's still alive?" I was surprised and understood how Faolan was worse than war. He would be the cause of it.

"I did not end his life, no," Zephyr answered. "I wish I would have, but I was in his territory, claiming that which was not mine. Technically, at the time, you were a Crow and in his lands. By all rights, you were of his ownership. And before you yell at me, I know no one owns you, but Elphame law doesn't care how you feel."

My stomach flopped. "I wish you had killed him."

"As do I, but I'd have caused a war," Zephyr explained and gripped my hand. "You are worth all the wars in all the world, little Crow, but had we gone to war in his land, I fear we wouldn't have gotten our people out of other territories in time. They would have died. And our war would not only be with Faolan. He would also have lost countless innocents in a battle not of their making. We must think of innocent lives when edging the prospects of war."

I squeezed his hand in return. "You made the right choice, Zeph."

Solas growled from his end of the table. "We should have taken the risk and killed him where he stood. We could have protected the innocent. The war is coming anyway. We could have started one and finished one by now."

I laughed a little until I realized he was dead serious. "Are you going to meet him?"

"He is requesting both of us, Perdi, you and me," Solas answered. "If you cannot do it or would rather not, I will not force you. I will simply decline. He can't force you to meet. I could go to see what he wants and come back and let you know. It is your decision. I, like you, will not be owned or commanded about."

"A truce or peace, though... Is that not worth something?" I asked. "It sounds like such a rare occurrence in Elphame."

"Yes, it's worth it," Zephyr answered.

"No, it's not," Solas answered.

I frowned. "Which one is it, boys? Yes or no?"

"Yes," Zephyr answered and glared at Solas. "We need time to get our people to safety. This buys us the time we need. Too many will die a needless death if we do not accept it. I'm sorry, Perdi, but their lives aren't worth your discomfort. I would ask you to grin and bear it. It is not the worst fate you've already suffered here."

"If it's worth it, we will go," I answered after weighing the options over. "Zeph is right. Seeing Faolan again is not worse than what I've already endured. It's probably the easiest thing I've been asked to do so far." I paused for a moment and let the initial fear roll through me. "Can I have a Sluagh or something? I think I'd feel better if I had a dragon beside me. Maybe something that bites."

"Like a pet? Are you going to put it next to your gargoyle when we get back?" Solas laughed. "We will bring them if that makes you feel better."

"I bite, and I'll be at your side." Zephyr grinned, and it was anything but friendly. "He will not take you again, little Crow. I give my word. For that, there would be wars that trembled the earth. Even the Gods would come to watch the massacre."

I smiled. "You're such a flirt."

He leaned in, his eyes darting from Solas to me playfully. "Could you not say that so loudly? Your Little King, here, may get jealous."

"You're ridiculous." I laughed and pushed him away.

"I've been told I'm somewhat of a catch."

"When do we leave?" I asked and ignored Zephyr, to his own amusement.

"This evening, before dinner," Solas answered.

"He wants to meet on Courtless Lands? I take it he doesn't know they are yours?" I asked.

"No one knows," Solas answered. "But they will soon find out."

I ate my breakfast and watched them discuss the particulars of the meeting. They sent word to the Dark Courts to return home or go into hiding if they were too far from the Dark Territories. Those who needed aid to return would be helped. I watched them go back and forth, with Zephyr always coming back to us just killing Faolan and making it home in time for dinner on the veranda. Solas, on the other hand, wanted to draw it out and make him squirm.

"I have a few ideas of my own." I spoke up. Faolan was a holder of truth, and my gut flared at the thought of him being killed. I knew, eventually, I would need to hear his truths. They were both more than willing to listen to my cunning ways.

* * * *

The Court of Less was not abandoned as all had thought. It was ruled by the Dark Court, Solas and every monster that made you keep the light on while you slept. And in these Dark Lands, nightmares were real and crashed through the night. Solas was Elphame's worst nightmare, and we stood on *his* land with *his* people and watched Faolan and his two men enter a territory they really shouldn't be in.

"Zeph, when you and Solas were fighting, your first day back, you mentioned a woman you cared for, the one you threatened to kill Solas to protect. Doesn't she worry about you when you play war games with Solas? I would."

"Then you've just answered your own question," he replied and glanced down. "You're the only other I've cared for."

"You'd kill Solas to protect me?"

"Oh, he'd do worse things than kill a king for you." Solas turned with a smile. "As would I. Are you ready to play said war games?"

I nodded. "As ready as I'll ever be."

Zephyr and I stood behind Solas. Zephyr had helped me pick 'a statement outfit'—or that's what he called it, a phrase he'd obviously picked up from Elswyth. I wore something between skimpy and if darkness could be contained in the fabric. He said, if anything, I'd be a reminder of what Faolan wanted and couldn't have. For kings, it was the worst form of torment. Zephyr strapped cold iron to my leather-clad thighs, along with the very knife I killed the Golden King with and pulled my hair back from my face. He mirrored my outfit, only his cleavage wasn't pushed into his throat, and he had to leave his weapons for the meeting. Solas, in his usual fashion, was dressed in casual black slacks and a white button-down shirt that snapped loose in the wind.

Faolan stood with two of his people, two who hadn't died at my hand. The one on his right stared into my eyes for much longer than the other had. The air around him was cold. The very grass under his feet had grown frosted. He hadn't a weapon, but I knew he, like Zephyr, was a weapon all on his own. The edge of his mouth lifted as he fought not to grin. He lifted his brows once and stared off, bored, I imagined, of the games of kings.

The agreement made was for a truce during the meeting. Neither would strike out against the other. It was simple enough, and Solas had every intention of letting Faolan sink himself. Kings always did, I was told. Power corrupts the mind and turns kings foolish.

"Little King." Solas was the first to speak. "You've interrupted our day. Tell me, what could be so important that you'd stand with the very nightmares that haunt your dreams?"

Faolan smiled politely. It was unnerving how calm he was. "Thank you for coming."

"Why are you here?" I asked. "You're either brave or stupid—and I'm beginning to think the latter."

The one to his right pursed his lips and tried not to laugh. He held my stare for longer than was comfortable. Something about him said he wasn't scared of the song and dance. He looked like he had done it too many times to care for these games. I envied his position. To be so used to this, it bothered him not.

"I have spoken with the Unseelie and Seelie Courts. We agree to allow the Crow…" Faolan started, and Zephyr's growl drained the color from Faolan's face.

"Perdi... Perdita... Miss Darkmore... We agree to allow her to return to her people, the mortal realm."

I fought to laugh at his fear. It wasn't funny, but it was certainly satisfying. "Miss Darkmore...that will do."

"And why would you agree to this?" Solas asked.

"We feel she, Miss Darkmore, has thrown the balance off in Elphame. Her being here has been chaos. She brings death on her heels. The Golden King, the new king, has agreed not to seek retribution for the slaying of his father if she agrees to return and never come back."

"What about the oath? If she were to leave, the oath would be broken, and the mortal realm would suffer greatly," Zephyr asked. "Her leaving would mean the death of her people."

"The oath will be considered fulfilled," Faolan answered.

"That's a generous offer," Solas said and turned to me. "Isn't that a generous offer?"

"Yes, I'd say that is more than generous." I looked at Zephyr. "Wouldn't you agree?"

Zephyr nodded. "More than what I would give in any bargain."

Solas crossed his arms. "For such a lavish gift, I wonder what the cost would be? Elphame gives nothing without getting something you do not want to give in return."

I stepped forward. "What about the Taking of future Crows?"

"We are willing to renegotiate," Faolan answered.

"The answer, then, is no. It either stops, or I will not agree to those terms," I answered.

Faolan's face flushed. "No one would agree to that, Perdi. There will always be a Crow, as there will always be a Gate. The powers of Elphame would never allow the tithe to end. There is not a power alive that can stop the Taking from happening."

"No," I answered. "You have my answer."

"You've heard the lady." Solas' jaw clenched. I could feel the heat billowing off him. "Good day, gentlemen."

Faolan grabbed my arm and yanked me into his chest. "You must leave, and you must leave now. You have no idea what you're about to do, Perdi. You won't end this. This will be the beginning of a world we cannot possibly survive. You will start something you won't be able to end." His fingers dug into my arms, then he flinched. "I can smell him on you."

"Get your hands off me."

Zephyr's shadows erupted out of him in all directions. Tendrils of black crawled through the air like beasts. The very earth knew well enough to bow down to the nightmares unfolding and shook under our feet. Everything for miles had understood what it meant when Zephyr raged—everything but Faolan. The shadows crawled up my body and pushed against Faolan until he let go or faced the wrath I let loose from the basement of the Golden Courts. Faolan's grip went slack, and I stepped back to Solas.

Solas had already burst into a pit of burning rage. The anger pulsed off him in waves that blew against us all. Steam poured from his body and sizzled in the air. If Zephyr were shadows, Solas was the very night. "You come into *my* court and abuse *my* guest, *my* Crow? Touch her again, and you will lose those fucking hands moments before your head."

"*Your* court?" Faolan laughed. "These are Courtless Lands."

The Sluagh melted from the tree lines, crawling on too many legs and bellies. The sky darkened with their presence. The ground rumbled as Faolan's stupidity had woken beasts who hadn't tasted war in eons and were starved. To my left, a Sluagh landed with the force of the world behind him. On his shoulder, Orrian stood proud. A small sash of red hung on her shoulders. If you looked close enough, you'd see it was wet in blood. The owner of that blood I didn't know and didn't ever want to ask. I stared ahead to Faolan and smiled.

Solas' voice was uncomfortably calm, the way the sea calmly pulled out before smashing your village to pieces. "These lands are Dark Court. To protect them from the evil within this realm, I have hidden them and who watches over them. I hid away the darkness, but rest assured, Little King, these are the Dark Courts, and you are in *my* territory."

"You stand in darkness, Little King, with the Aos Si." Zephyr stepped forward, his shadows slowly crawling back. He stood by his king. I watched as every muscle engaged, ready, waiting for Faolan to make one wrong move, blink in a threatening way or reach for me again. "Count your blessings that we have been asked to leave your heart where it remains. But the evening is still young enough for them to change their minds."

"The Aos Si have been gone for decades," Faolan said, but his movement betrayed him. Both he and his men backed up as they realized who I had released in the Golden Courts.

"We are not gone and most certainly aren't forgotten." Zephyr grinned. "The Aos Si fight only in righteous wars. So, I'd ask yourself, is it a good thing to see us now?"

Faolan pointed at me and shook his head. "You have no idea what you're doing, Perdi. Their blood will be on your hands. This doesn't end just because you want it to. You may close one door, but you'll open up the very pits of hell, and no one will live through what it spits out. By the time you realize what you've done, it'll be too late, and we'll all be dead. You'll be dead, Perdi."

I channeled the anger and hurt and let it flow through me. It danced across my skin, the parts of me that had been torn apart because of him. It felt so bloody good to have the object of my bottomless pool of hate standing before me. He was my target and only him. Every road and path that had bloodied my soul led back to him. I ate up the power in the air and pushed it out to Faolan. I brought him and his men to their knees. There would be no payment for this show of magick. I wasn't taking it from the Goddess. I took it freely from the air, from Solas and his people.

"If you're not careful, you'll die long before me," I replied and felt the ground move as dozens of Sluagh fell from the sky to land at my back. Faolan tried to stand and reach for me at the same time, but Solas was faster than Faolan's fear and pushed him back to his knees. "Faolan, this is your last day of freedom. Do not make it your last breath."

Faolan shook his head, and a sad smile pulled at his lips. "Take it, because you'll sentence us all to graves long before we were meant to fall."

Zephyr leaned down and smiled the same way a monster did before it ate your children for breakfast. "You were warned, Little King, how you would suffer if you touched her. Yet, here we are, her smell fresh upon your flesh, again. How I will enjoy carving it off you. And with your very last breath, you will curse the Gods for having known my name."

"You can't do this! There will be war!" Faolan screamed. He clutched at his belt, finding his empty sheath, his weapons taken off for the meeting. He was foolish, his head too high. We had left our weapons as he had, but Solas and Zephyr were war on two legs. They *were* the weapons we were bringing.

"There will always be war, Faolan." Solas stepped away from him and stood at my back.

"Show him to his new cell." I looked at Zephyr. "And make sure he gets there in one piece. He is, after all, a wedding gift for a very dear friend."

Solas and I turned and walked into the thickness of Sluagh. I didn't flinch when I heard Faolan scream my name. I didn't turn back when I heard the growl of the Sluagh.

"You could have left," Solas whispered as we walked away.

"No, I couldn't." I grabbed his hand. And there, I sealed my fate. I would die for Elphame, as I would die for my people. The Sluagh, who had landed at my side, shuffled on the earth behind us. "I don't get to keep him, do I?"

Solas laughed. "They will always come if you call. But no, you can't keep him."

Chapter Nine

Dread settled against my bones in the halls of the Dark Court. Magick tugged at my core, the kind of magick that pushed me to keep walking for fear of death. But I had felt real fear before. I had bathed in it and choked it down for months. This, what now coated the air, was nothing more than smoke and mirrors, small parlor tricks in a place that dealt with dread so pure that men and women killed themselves to avoid it. Today, I ate it down like sweet jam. From my bedroom, I walked the halls, seeking whatever wanted not to be found or seen, and while I stood outside the door to Solas' office, I found what wished to be hidden.

"You've cost us everything." Her voice slid from under the door, barely audible, muffled by layers of magic. "You put the Dark Courts in danger, Solas, risked everything."

"It was a calculated risk." His response, even muted behind the magick, was calmer than hers.

"Decades, Solas, of hiding your ownership of the Court of Less, and you threw it away for nothing."

"It wasn't for nothing. It would have come out eventually." A loud bang and growl followed. "I did it on my terms, my way. I'm not your puppet to command."

"I desperately hope you're right, or everything I've worked so hard for was for naught. We've sacrificed countless lives and power for this…this Crow."

"*This* Crow?" Solas' tone heated. "Don't start. She is more than a Crow. She says she'll help, and I believe her."

Her laughter rubbed against my head like cat claws. "Oh, she says she'll help *you*? And what if she decides she will not? What then, Solas? What big plans do you have for your court when you fail?"

"Then she will not help," he shouted.

"No, Solas. That will not be the end of it. This is her fate. War is coming in her name, and many will die for her. Make every life worth it, Solas. I will not see our people slaughtered because of your little Crow."

I stepped away when the room shook, and books fell to the floor. The dread thickened, but it wasn't magick that created the sick feeling in the pit of my stomach. It was the truth that sent shivers down my spine. I tiptoed from his office and the argument about me. My fate was entwined with Elphame and countless souls who depended on me. Solas, still protecting me, had done his best to shield me from the horrible truth and the cold, harsh reality his people faced.

I found Zephyr outside, sitting cross-legged in the shadows. I had watched him on many nights, stepping into the forest in the dark, surrounded by just his shadows. I knew as I stepped into the darkness that I'd be welcomed like an old friend. He would know it was me, long before I had even decided to search for him. My pearl would tell him all he needed to know.

I took a seat at his back and leaned into him. "Who is Solas arguing with?"

"His priestess," Zephyr answered but tensed at the mention of her.

"Who is she to him? You only really argue like that with people you know and care for."

Zephyr nodded in agreement. "Like mortals with their priests and church, she is his priestess. She guides him in all things, whether we want to see them or not."

"Why haven't I met her?"

"Because she is not *your* priestess, is she?" Zephyr answered in his usual blunt fashion.

"She's angry Solas outed himself as the king of the Court of Less. Why?"

Zephyr turned sideways and leaned his body into mine. "There are some things that are not meant to be known, Perdi. Some things are better left to the Fates to decide upon, and not little, snooping Crows. He confides in his priestess, and those confidences are not yours to know, or he'd tell you himself."

I leaned against him, glad for the silence that only his shadows could bring. "I'm always the last to know anything in this place."

"Be glad you're not the first to find out, the first they come to. For once, be glad you're just a Crow to most Fae and beneath approach. This world kills warriors and bards alike. It drowns the babies of temperamental mothers and strangles those who flinch at their cries. But if they don't think you're of any importance, you'll be one of the last to die," he answered. His sigh rippled through the shadows. "If you can't eat the monsters, Perdi, just stand at the back and wait for scraps."

"You're so poetic, Zeph." I smiled. "She told Solas that war is coming, in my name."

"It is always coming, Perdi. In whose name they march doesn't matter once you're on the battlefield. They'll either curse your name for it or cheer. But they will still be on that field, no matter whose name falls from their lips."

"I don't trust her," I answered for no particular reason. "Something in my gut tells me she is not where I should put my trust. But fear, yes, I should fear her."

"She doesn't need *your* trust, little Crow. She's not your priestess."

"I don't want to die in this godforsaken place," I whispered.

He hugged me from the side and kissed the top of my head the way a father or brother would. "None of us want to die, but the fates don't care what we want, do they? We're both living proof of that little joke. We're both everything we never wanted to be."

"You don't like who you are?"

"I like *who* I am, but *what* I am is a different story," he replied. "Like you, this place made me fight for each day I've had. That tends to leave a stain on the soul."

I understood completely what he meant. Elphame had turned us both into tools, and both of us railed against it, kicking and screaming. "The fates made the wrong choice when they picked me to champion their cause."

"Fate is the last page in every story, and it is only then that we will know how we earned such as destiny. Only the Gods and Goddesses know the moves we'll make. And no matter the choices made, we always end up going where we were meant to turn up."

"This, Zeph, is all I've ever been. From being born to become a Crow to fulfilling that destiny. My story has been riddled with fear of the unknown, pain from the known and a promise of more. What kind of joke am I to the Gods, for a single soul to be given such a burden? Surely, I haven't lived enough years to have earned a punishment like this."

"If I could, I would save you from your destiny, little Crow, from what you were created for. But I can make it easier for you."

"How?" I asked.

"I will be there. You won't walk your path alone."

I smiled and closed my eyes. "And I will be there for you, Zeph, for as long as the fates allow."

And for the briefest of moments, I felt him soften as if that was the very first time someone had offered to walk his path with him. A lonely life he must have had.

"A lonely life it was," he whispered, and I tensed. "I have your pearl. And in my shadows, with me beside you, it's difficult for you to keep truths to yourself. I can hear your thoughts, the ones with the greatest emotions attached."

"Soul-Eater," I grumbled.

"Little Crow," he answered. Without seeing him, I knew he was smiling.

"Let me stay here for a few more moments?" I asked. "It's the only place in the world where I am not a Crow, and no one wants something from me."

"It is why I come here, Perdi. I am no one here. I am nothing here. And sometimes, that means everything."

"You're not no one to me. No matter how tightly you wind yourself in these shadows, you're the only one who doesn't ask the world from me." I breathed in the faint scent in the air and smiled. "You smell of baked bread and clover. But behind all that, you smell like the forest and flowers and gardens."

"You can smell my memories of better days," he answered. "It's what I think of when the world hands me tasks most others would run from."

"They're not even my memories, but they calm me as if they were."

"And you, little Crow, always smell of the ocean, the saltiness of tears still to come. You smell of wars I've fought and ones still to come."

* * * *

It took hours for all of Elphame to know that the Court of Less was under the protection of the Dark Courts, and Solas was king of all that ate the night. Before the day bled away to the night, Solas' secret was out, and all Elphame curried for favor. It took even less time for Faolan to break under the pressure of Solas and the nightmares the Court of Shadows was known for. An hour after Faolan was taken, he told Solas that the new Golden King, Theofanis, had plans to rule all courts and, with that power, would invade the mortal realm. Theofanis decreed the oaths had been broken by the Crow, aided by the Dark Court. The Golden King, no different than his father, had started taking Royals hostage, killing off leaders of other families, of those who stood against him. In a matter of weeks, Theofanis had shown that he was worse than his father and would ensure his name was written in the books of history on the wickedest of pages.

Zephyr stood in full gear, ready for a battle we all knew would come. He filled the room as only he could. He was the very definition of frightening. "The Seelie and Unseelie know."

I stepped into the living room right as Zephyr finished his sentence. "They know what?"

"Of the Gate, the plan to close the Gate," he answered. "It's why they offered you your freedom."

"I take it they're not going to let me just march into the Gate. They're going to try to kill me first?" I asked but didn't need to look at either of them to know I'd be tracked all the way to the Gate. Nothing in Elphame was ever easy.

"I've sent scouts already, and we've increased patrols, but, Solas, they'll be coming harder than ever before. Anyone brave enough to come will do so. You know what we must do."

"War," I whispered, hearing the thuds on the roof. For hours, Gargoyles had been landing. I looked up at the dust falling from the ceiling. A new one had just arrived. "They're already here, Zeph."

Zephyr was gone, wrapped in shadows and purpose. Solas grabbed for my hand, and I pulled back. "Solas, get your people to safety. I can't remain here in the Dark Courts if you are willing to let your people die for me."

"I can't just leave you here unprotected." He grabbed for me again.

"We have no choice, Solas. Go. I will be fine." I pushed him to leave me. I watched as he was torn between his people and me. He couldn't lead from the back. He had to be at the front. He had to show them the horror of the Dark Courts, or he'd never protect his people. He'd never get me to the Gate alive.

Solas kept his eye on me, but I knew he was listening to the violence outside. Screams erupted around the house and in the trees. An army had come to the very door of Solas' home. His people, both weak and strong, were fighting for my freedom, my life. I would not hide, protected, in these walls. No one would die for me while I stayed cloistered in my room. The days for shelter were gone. The days of hiding had passed. The time for war was now.

"I'm not alone," I called to him and ran for my bedroom, to the safety of the gargoyles—those who sat with me every night until my screaming stopped, those who gave me the truth in the harshest of ways. I had very few friends in Elphame, but I'd count them as part of that group of people who would protect me. Seth, the one who came most often, who slept at the head of my bed, was waiting.

"You are very much not alone." Seth, my friend, my protector, *mine,* stood ready at the ledge of the house, his wings wide and ready. "Fly, little Crow. Let us punish those who have foolishly come to break your wings."

I climbed onto the rail of my balcony, and without hesitation, I dove, arms wide, without fear, and he caught me before I could hit the ground. Four gargoyles followed. They flanked me left and right. I would not go without a fight. Elphame took me once, and I didn't fight, but not this time. They wanted a Crow, and they would get one on the wings of hell. This Crow would fly into the very arms of war.

To the north, Zephyr and his shadows rolled through the trees, falling everything in their path. Blades smashed against each other. Weak and bloody screams sounded their demise. I sent up a prayer that those last pleas were not from the grounds I now called home. To the south, Solas moved like a raging river, tearing down everything that tried in vain to stop him. His darkness rolled across the earth and ate those it could touch.

Seth dropped me to the ground, and I rolled to a stop. Clusters of warriors moved through the trees, silent. But I knew the song of the court, the movements, how it ebbed and flowed. I had spent night after night listening to every creak and crash. I knew every leaf outside my window. I closed my eyes and listened to a forest that knew me as I knew it.

To my left and right, they glided toward me on a wind that was High Fae. I could feel their power in the wind like dust. It tasted of their belief that they were unstoppable. I pushed my magick out. I finally opened the door that I knew I'd never close again. I unleashed all my Malice and held nothing back. She exploded from me the way it burst from Zephyr. This time she was controlled but starved. She sought and saw all. It knew my opponent's every move. It hungered for death. I took one glance around for those I'd wish not to kill before I pulled the magick from the air. I pulled every drop into my soul, and I ate those who had been foolishly brave enough to invade. I drank them down like a fine wine and rolled them over my tongue, seeking their truths as I swallowed. They had come for me and thought they'd get me without a fight. They were sent with death on their minds. There was no offer of peace. They would kill me if they could. But they knocked on the wrong door. What monsters feared lived in these dark woods. *Fools.*

I walked through the trees, my arms tight at my sides and head tilted to the sound of men falling to the ground. The men who shouldn't have come would now pay the ultimate price for following a leader who would have me dead. One after another, they fell to the ground, dried shells of who they had once been. Around me, people ran, shrieking. The intruders were not all they feared. I had become another nightmare of the Dark Court. As fire poured off me and licked the ground where I stood, they all ran. They wouldn't get far.

Zephyr was suddenly on me, throwing me to the ground and breaking my hold on my Malice. He wrapped us in his shadows, a brick wall to the world outside. Through the air, arrows whistled their approach, sinking into the ground around us, aimed at me.

"Run!" he yelled into my ear.

"You run," I answered and pulled myself from under him. "Run, Zeph, or you will die with them. I don't have your or Solas' control."

"Leave not a single one alive. If you do this, if you take them, they all must die. Everyone dies to keep what you've done a secret." His answer was left on the wind as he vanished into the shadows and hunted from the dark.

I ran through the trees as if I had grown up in that forest. I ran toward them, toward death. I didn't want to die. No, just the opposite. I ran toward a life that was rightfully mine, a life I had earned to keep. I didn't hold back. I couldn't. Fate had given me a path that was covered in blood and bones, and I had to fight for every inch I gained. But it was *my* path, *my* life, *my* right to walk it, even if I had to crawl over the broken bodies to get where I knew I was needed. Sometimes we had to leave home in order to protect it. And I would burn this world to a crisp to do so.

From deep within, I let the fire go. I let it out without the fierce control I had always gripped around it. I focused my fear and pushed it into the blaze, igniting the curse I knew I was. I would become the blight on this world, as I had promised, where only one equaled my terror—Zephyr.

I let go of my pain, let it fuel my fire and burn under its flames. I screamed as I ate the Seelie and Unseelie who were in my path, who weren't smart enough to run. I drained those who dared step foot into the darkness, a land that welcomed my broken soul. I didn't stop until the screams ended and the only sound left was my heart pounding, the only life left in my wake. At my feet, soot from the fire within me covered the ground, mixed with bones and cooked bits of clothes from an army that didn't win, that would never win. My rage had burned the needles and leaves and charred the earth where I stepped. With each one I had taken, I took back that which belonged to no one else—my life, my freedom.

"You can come with your armies until you have no one left to send, but you will only ever leave with their bones," I called out into the dark forest. I dropped to my knees, blood running from my nose. "The cost is mine."

* * * *

"You just had to show me up, didn't you?" Zephyr taunted me.

I smiled weakly, curled on my side, covered in a blanket of darkness. The price of my magick, as dark as it had been, had been worth it. "I live to see you look bad in front of the ladies."

"I felt what you did, little Crow," Zephyr whispered for only me to hear.

"I ate their magick," I answered and felt no guilt.

"You ate their souls," he answered.

I frowned. "No, I ate their magick, their lives."

"It's the same thing. You ate their souls. Worry not. Your secret is safe with me."

"What secret?" I asked.

He leaned. "Soul-Eater."

"No…" I answered and stared at him. "How?"

"It is why you heard me behind the wall in the Golden Court and how you can call on my shadows, whether I will it or not. I have your pearl, Perdi, and it tastes like home," Zephyr replied. "And each time you anger, I watch the temptation play in the back of your mind, the darkness tempting you to do your worst. My darkness is attracted to the darkness in you."

"Attracted? I don't think so, Zeph. You're a nice guy, and I know you care about me, but…"

He barked a laugh. "Not like that. My darkness is fascinated with you. You are the only other like me. As curious as I am, and my shadows, it is not a romantic interest. We, my shadows and I, are merely seeking a home, familiarity, someone like us. We're all looking for that place that's so safe that we don't have to hide who we are, where we don't have to pretend that we're someone or something else."

"I don't know if I should say sorry? Most times, I'm only thinking of them, and they show up. Only once did I mean to do it, the day I gave you one of my pearls."

"No, don't be sorry. Your pull on my shadows is a small thing, more irritating than anything else. I'm not used to it. You'll learn how to control your call to me, but it'll take time. When I came into maturity, my control was so bad that I ate an entire village of souls. That you're calling to things already dead is a minor thing." He grinned. "I wish I was joking."

"How is it that I pay like this, but you seem just fine?"

"Because you're using your mortal magick rather than your Fae abilities. Don't fret. It gets easier. You are brand new. You are also a mortal. I'm not. You'll learn, and I'll be there to guide you."

"Perdi!" Solas' voice boomed through the halls and shook my bones.

"We will discuss this later. I'd advise you to keep this little tidbit to yourself. Soul-Eaters have been hunted to near extinction for a good reason. Two of us, and they'll burn the world to find us."

"Thank you for getting me home, Zeph."

"I'll always get you home." He stood and smiled, a smile that reached his eyes as I realized what I had said. With a wink, he was gone, wrapped in his shadows.

Home. This was home. Solas was home. I had been searching for a place, but it wasn't a place I had been looking for or needed. The Dark Court was where I felt at peace with my brokenness. My sharp pieces didn't stand out here. We were all jagged and broken here.

Solas came through the door like a storm, his night wind trailing behind him. His face relaxed once he saw me safe, unharmed. As soon as his hands touched me, the fire inside my stomach died, and I was able to breathe. He was the cool touch to my burning grasp. We needed each other for balance, as the sun needed the moon. The cost flowed through me, into him and out into the darkness. He ate my pain willingly.

"You were always home." I held his face in my hands. "I've been looking for *you*, not a place, but you."

"When I saw you jump from your balcony, I thought…" He shuddered against me. "I thought you were ending your life to save us all."

"I'd never…" I started, and he put his fingers to my lips.

"But then I saw you fly. I watched as you dove and became a Crow. You were fighting for us. I thought, if you died, you'd die protecting my people. And at first, I wanted to shield you, protect you, but knew that if I did, I'd stop who you are becoming."

"And who is that?" I asked.

"Who you were always meant to be, a Crow who suffered for none. You were born to be free, and I was born to find you." Solas kissed my mouth softly. "No matter what comes or who comes, I won't ever let them take you from me. There is no war I fear more than I fear the loss of you. I would stand against all, alone, before I gave you up."

My heart broke for him. A lifetime of searching for me, holding me, only to lose me. As a child, I was taught that death came for all equally, but I knew the harsh truth of it. It snatched at anyone it could, cutting people down who deserved more time. It took those who were far too young and left behind those who were old and had lived more lives than the rest. Death took the good and left the vile, those who were deserving of the cruelest of endings. Tonight, in the arms of Solas, I felt the harsh glare of death as he sat down in the corner and waited for me.

"For one night, let us be here, in this very moment, and forget about what led us here and what is yet to come," I asked. "I need to close it out, just for one night."

"I would give anything to make this go away for you," he answered.

"Then kiss me." I smiled, and he did.

Tonight, we made love. Because soon, I'd have no more tonights. We'd wage a war that would take them all away. I'd leave no witnesses if that's what it took to get to the Gate. But even if I did, I wouldn't be here to deal with the fallout. Solas would, and he'd be alone again. Knowing what fate had shoved through our door left my heart a little more broken today than yesterday. I had finally found him, the one I would die for. And now, I'd be called to task. It would be my final sacrifice, a demand of every Crow before me.

Chapter Ten

I'd seen my death countless times, and each time I did, I moved a little closer to the dying light. The more I inched closer, the calmer my soul became. The flickering light, barely holding on for me, was waiting for a sacrifice that both it and my soul knew I'd make. In every dream for the last two weeks, it ended with me willingly giving my life to the Gate. There had been no other outcome I'd choose and none I'd want to make.

I dreamed of Elda's visions of me but never of me being trapped in Elphame alive. It was always of my dead and bloodied body on the grass outside of the Gate. It was so real. I could feel the earth under my shoulders and smell what the war had left lingering in the air. Only now did I realize I was watching my end before it came. Any question I had remaining of my fate was washed away. I would die in Elphame, and I wasn't as scared as I thought I'd be. It was hard to fear a fate you knew was coming and couldn't be changed—an ending I didn't want to change. Solas had given his entire life to end the Taking. This would be my gift to him. He would have the rest of his days without the horrors of becoming a monster, over and over. Once he accepted the pain of my leaving, he'd finally be free—and so would I.

I walked through the trees of the Dark Court with death following closely behind me. Gone was my hate and my anger. It had burned away the night of the attempted invasion. It had been replaced with a certain quietness that hadn't been there before. And with it, I was able to look to my future and watch it slowly come to a close. I was uncertain what would happen after, when I died, or where I'd go for what I had done to survive. But I was calm in knowing I didn't regret it. Like my mother, I'd die without many regrets. Up until her final moments, she had none. The Guardians hanged her for being a witch, killed her for dark magick. It broke my father, but I knew that if the Fates allowed it, he was with her right now. And they'd both be waiting for me.

I suppose, in a way, I'd get what I had fought so hard to gain. I'd be seeing my family again. Soon, I'd leave. I would step into the fog willingly, and I wouldn't come back out. I'd close the Gate and seal my fate. My death. That thought, death, had once eased me to sleep at night. One day, Elphame would kill me, and I'd finally be at peace. I had yearned for my last breath, however painful it would be. Now, it hurt. Not the idea of death, but knowing Solas would be alone again. All his life, he waited for me, never knowing he was waiting to dig a hole for me. I hurt for him, not for myself. For him, my heart broke, and I wished I could convince Fate to choose someone else.

Tomorrow, the Dark Court would wage war on the waiting armies. Hundreds of thousands of Fae waited for me and me alone. I would stand on the battlefield with Solas, and we'd go to war, not against anyone, but for all our people to finally have peace. But it would take a brutal battle to gain that peace. If I made it to the Gate alive, I'd die in the end. If I didn't make it to the Gate, I'd die just the same. There were no alternatives that didn't result in my death and the deaths of countless others. If I tried not, innocents would pay a price I was always meant to bear. If I gave up, the mortal world would suffer. The decision was as easy as it was difficult.

The Darkmore line had been fated with this task long ago. The moment we'd opened the Gate, my destiny had been decided for me. And now that it was upon me, I didn't fear it. It was coming full circle, a balance in all things. But I'd be lying if I said I hadn't cursed my line for handing me such a painfully short future.

Zephyr stepped out from the tree line to find me sitting on a log, eating my lunch. "We are to be training for the Gate, not having a picnic."

"You know, the last time I had a picnic, I fed two servants to water nymphs." I looked up with a smile.

"Riiight." He dragged the word out. "You freed two slaves. You'll never be as cold as you try to be with me. Remember, I have your pearl and the many memories that come with it."

"That's not a comforting thought." I shuddered.

"The truth isn't meant to be one way or the other. It just is."

"Well then, this could be my last chance at having a picnic. Would you really take that away from a dying girl?" I smiled. "Plus, I packed you a lunch as well."

"Your confidence in tomorrow is encouraging." He smiled and took a seat beside me. "But I could eat."

"For a Dark Court, it is prettier than I thought it would be." I stared off into the trees and life around us.

"And the Golden Court isn't as beautiful as you'd think. At one time, the courts truly were what they were called. The Golden Court, all of Seelie, was pure, and every Fae wanted to be there, to be a part of the shining courts. It truly was a sight to see. Even to be a lesser Fae of the Seelie Court was better than High Fae of the Unseelie Courts. As new kings came and went, it shifted. Now it is only magick that keeps the appearance. It's why it looks beautiful but feels awful. The Seelie Courts, however pretty they appear, hold a darkness that makes this place look peaceful."

"It's more than that, Zeph. There's a calmness here that can't be found elsewhere."

"It helps that you're not being tortured here," he answered, and I glanced over. "Sorry. I didn't mean to dredge up painful shit."

I shrugged it off. "We've all got baggage. Mine is no worse than yours."

"But yours is still raw. Mine is long-callused. There isn't much that can call up my pain anymore."

"That's sad," I replied and felt a twinge of pity for him. To be of a people who created so much pain, you just got used to it.

"Are we going to discuss my pains and hurts, or are we going to train? Because I didn't come here for a cure of all that ails my soul. We don't have the time to talk of them all, and I don't have the will to tear open wounds, long healed," he said, readying to pack in his lunch. Avoidance was crucial to survival for both mortals and Fae alike.

"How's the planning going?" I asked and bit into an apple. The flavor reminded me of Nix's garden, his little hands pruning and picking off dead leaves. He'd spent countless hours tending to every inch of my yard, top to bottom. What had started as my mother's herb garden had grown into a massive plot of greenery. Flowers and vegetables and fruits had filled my kitchen table throughout the year. Even in the winter, he had grown frost-craving plants.

Zephyr lifted his head. "He's home, Perdi. He just got back before I came here. He's waiting for you to come home."

"Who?"

"Nix. That's who you were thinking of."

"Can you read my mind?" I stared at him and blushed.

"No, and I'm grateful for that, with how you and Solas carry on. I could only imagine the scandalous things you think." He teased with a wink. "I can feel you…your pearl. When you think of Nix, it's a particular feeling you get, like when you open your favorite book or smell a scent from your childhood. When you think of him, you smell like apples. Each person triggers a smell or feeling in us all. With Solas, your swirling mind comes to a crawl. It's like the world could be ablaze, and you'd be the only one smiling because of him. When you think of him, you smell like lavender and feel like hope."

"Do you always feel what I'm feeling?" I asked.

"Yes, but I feel you more than any other because of who we are. But adding your pearl to the mix, I can feel you as if I'm experiencing it all myself. Let's not talk about what I feel when you're in bed with Solas."

I rolled my eyes. "So, the planning… You were about to tell me."

"There's not much to say. It is a war, like every other one gone by and still to come. Our people have been taken to safety, and those who will fight have kissed their families and are waiting to die."

"Now who sounds like the fountain of encouragement?" I replied.

"It is not meant to be, little Crow. Many will die. It is a truth we all know and accept. It is the reality of war, and no one is free from it. The moment each of us steps onto that battlefield, we all accept we may not step back off. So, we do what we can in the time we have, we say goodbye to those we love, and we prepare to meet a fate that has already been decided by the Gods and Goddesses."

"But you'll come back. You always do," I added.

He nodded. "It is rare indeed that I wonder if this will be my last day. But the day will come, and I welcome the reason I'll give my life. Because that is the only way an army will stop me, if I willingly go to my death for someone else."

"Would you ever sacrifice yourself?" I asked.

"I'd give a lot to save Solas, but I know I'd never have to give my life for his. He, like me, won't die unless it is in the place of someone else. We're a tough lot. Death won't come easily for either of us. When it does knock on our door, it'll be to save someone we love." He tilted his head and shrugged. "I want to say no, that I wouldn't do such a thing. But I believe fate will make that decision for me long down the road. Rest easy. It will not be this war that takes me. There will not be enough men on that field to take either Solas or myself."

"How do I get to the Gate with everyone willing to die to stop me?" I asked.

"You trust in the fact that there are also people willing to die to get you there," he answered and pulled out a small, weathered map. "On the right side, this is where you're headed. Our very best will be there, all of Sluagh, Aos Si and those I would not wish to ever meet in battle. They will get you there, come hell or high water. There is no force on this earth that will tear them all from your side."

"Can't I just eat my way through?" I asked.

"Sure, if you want to use up all your energy and have nothing left for the Gate," he answered with a mocking tone. "You're not strong enough to try it, and we can't risk you blowing your only shot at this. Save everything you have until you get there. You'll feel the energy in the air, eat it and save it. Use it only when absolutely necessary. You asked once how I could do this and not pay for it like you. That is part of the reason why. I do not expend energy I do not freely have. I eat it wherever I go and always save a pool inside for when I can't."

"What happens if you run out?" I asked.

"I don't. Part of being a Soul-Eater is that I have shadows. They collect energy wherever they go. And if ever I were in dire need, I'd sacrifice my shadows. I'd eat all they are."

I nodded. "What exactly is a Soul-Eater?"

"Exactly what it sounds like. We can eat souls, use their magick and take away their will to live. We eat their very lives to sustain our own. It is not something I'd wish for you to be."

"Why were you hunted?"

"Because of what we can do, Perdi. It isn't something to be taken lightly. We can bleed them dry of everything they are," he answered. "The original Fae, those from the original court, were not called Soul-Eaters. We were the Finis. We were both cruelty and mercy, life and death, peace and war."

"Did you say Finis?" I asked.

"Yes. We are the Finis, those who helped usher you from this world to the next. We were there for the end of every Fae and ensured each soul was released to the Gods and Goddesses. But eventually, like all power, they became corrupt, greedy and abused their powers. They no longer cared for their duties as Finis and were hunted down and killed, labeled Soul-Eaters. There weren't many of us who survived. But I learned control from the Court of Blood and Bones. When I could, I left and suffered many losses. I was the only one to master that control and the only Finis to still have my life. Without control, your power can leach out and kill everyone you love. And when it comes back to collect its debt, it could take your life as payment."

"Elda, she called me..." I started, and Zephyr lifted his hand.

"Don't. We all have sat with Grandmother Elda, but none speak of what was said. That is yours and yours alone."

"But—" I started again, and he glared at me. "Okay."

"Truly, Perdi, should I know the details, it would change your path in my favor, which would alter my own path. I do not wish to play a game against Fate. I will lose, as will you. We do not meddle with her. She's one hell of a warrior and has won every battle to date," Zephyr warned. "To even try is pointless."

"So, Soul-Eaters, what about me? How do I get rid of it?" I asked.

He laughed. "You can't just get rid of it, little Crow."

The Crow comment made me smile. He never said it to be hateful, merely to show me how much younger I was than he. Of every Fae, Zephyr was never cruel—honest to a fault but never intentionally wicked, with me at least. Everyone else got a different version of him, and cruel did not cover who he could become.

"One from my line is likely mixed in yours. And the longer you remain in Elphame, the more Fae you become. You're Wildfey. It's the luck of the draw that's the Fae part of you that decided to awaken. Wildfey were mixed with too many others to know what Fae would be born. They really were wild at one time. They were owned by no court, or at least, no court willing to try to own one. You are very much wild, as were your ancestors. I pity the fools who believe they can tame you."

"The luck of the draw?" I asked.

"Being this, a Soul-Eater, it isn't a curse I'd wish on anyone. Not all born to a Soul-Eater will become one. It is only a very small percentage of Fae who are fated to become one. When we are born, we're watched for signs. If by some twisted hand you became one, you were sent away to train, sent away for fear of who you were becoming. It's a lonely road to walk and one you must walk with absolute care and attention to every single detail. One bad dream, one loss of control, one wish and you could be the cause of countless deaths and not even mean to do it." Zephyr's face told me more than his words could. He spoke from experience. He spoke from his memories.

"Will other parts wake up, too? I mean, am I going to all of a sudden sprout wings?"

He stared at me for longer than I wanted. "No, Perdi, you're not going to wake up with wings any more than I am."

"Sorry…stupid question."

"Normally, I'd say there wasn't such a thing, but yes, it was." He laughed. "You are who you are, and no amount of wishing is going to change that. We, you and I, are the last."

"Will the power grow?"

"Your hunger will. And the more you feed it, the stronger you'll become. You will never become what I am if that's what you're worried about. Both of my parents were Finis. You are only part, polluted from mortal blood. But even a shadow of who I am will tremble the world."

"And if I don't feed it?" I asked and ignored the polluted comment.

"I don't know. I'm a man of war. There's nothing but food for the taking. I've never met another of my kind who has not fed it. I've no idea what will happen. I don't recall hearing of it as a child, but a child's mind doesn't remember such things." He shrugged. "Decades, centuries, have passed, and I've only met those who hone their abilities like any other Fae. If I had to guess, I'd say you'd die. But I think your Malice will break her cage and do it to keep you alive."

"Would Solas ask me to leave because of this? Scared I'd eat his people?" I asked.

"Solas can never find out, Perdi. Two of us will attract the wrath of all Fae and will risk all his people.

He'd be stupid not to send us both out of his court. He couldn't just send you, uncontrolled, into the rest of Elphame. I'd be sent with you," he answered, and my stomach flipped. "For me to still exist is sheer will on my part and no longer because someone allowed me to live. Leading the Aos Si has made me difficult to come for, but that doesn't stop the challenges. Every single day, Perdi, is a fight for my life."

"I can't lie to him."

"I'm not telling you to lie. I'm telling you to keep it to yourself until we figure it out," he replied. "Don't force Solas to choose between protecting you and saving his people from war. You will never be able to live with the decision he'll make."

"He'll choose his people," I replied.

"I would have said the same thing a year ago. But not now, not after seeing him with you. For now, just keep your mouth shut."

"What are we figuring out? It's not like the threat will be long-lived." I pointed out my inevitable fate to die in Elphame. I couldn't be much of a threat from the grave.

"Just keep it to yourself for now. You don't understand. If the other courts found out that Solas housed two Soul-Eaters, the fight would never stop, regardless of whether you survived the Gate or not. They'd come, and you'd never even have the chance to close the Gate," he answered then froze. "Damn it. I have to go."

"You can't just drop this on me and leave, Zeph. What the hell is more important?"

"Hunting down the last of the survivors from the attack at the manor." He rubbed the bridge of his nose and let out a long and shaking breath. "Perdi, if there are any who survived the attack, they will tell others about what you did. If you're not held to blame, I will be. I told you to kill them all for a reason. I never leave survivors."

"Solas knew what I had done when I was on the run. He saw the bodies in the forest. Faolan knows what I did, too."

"That's easily explained with dark magick, wild from your emotion. You come from a potent line of witches. Last night, you killed over two hundred soldiers. Right now, Solas thinks it was me who did it. What do you think will happen if the rest of Elphame knows you can do that?"

"They'll kill me?"

He huffed a laugh. "No. Not even close. Soul-Eaters aren't that lucky. They'll refocus their attack and take you as they took me long ago. They will enter that battlefield not to kill you but to control you. They'll train you. They'll push you to become the new nightmare of Elphame. Then, when you're too broken to care, they'll loose you on the world. Do you want to be sent into the mortal world with this power and only hate as a focus?"

"No."

He stepped to my front. "And what happens if they send you back here? Or to a village of weaker Fae? What then, Perdi?"

I swallowed the lump in my throat. "I would never…"

"You will!" Zephyr shouted, getting his message across loud and clear. "You will, Perdi. You've only had a sip of what Elphame can do. You do not want to taste it all. The things they'll make you do? You don't want that life. Believe me. I've been there. I thought I was stronger than them all, but I wasn't. Pain and horror motivate us all in the worst of ways. No matter what you think you can endure, you will break. Even I broke, and I was trained to endure the worst."

"What the hell do I do, then?"

"Do not use it again unless you are backed into a corner with no way out. And if you do use it, be willing to kill everyone who saw it—and I truly mean everyone, Perdi. That is the cost of this power. There can *never* be survivors. If ever someone lives, you must be willing to hunt them to the ends of the earth. It's the harshest of truths to be a Soul-Eater, to choose your life over theirs. But those are the consequences we must face, each and every time we decide our lives are more important than theirs."

I nodded. "I've seen you use it. Why didn't you kill me? Why did you leave a witness?"

"I don't know," he answered and looked at me with wonder. He stayed paused, questioning why I still stayed above ground. "I must go."

"You're going to kill them if there are any left?" I asked. "Those who saw?"

"Yes. Or you and I will both be hunted. And I'd hate to show you what must be done to survive. I don't want that life for you. I hope you are never tasked with killing people who don't deserve it, just to protect who we are. There are times, little Crow, when witnesses don't deserve this fate, and it kills your soul to doll it out. Trust me when I tell you, the path we walk is rotten with pain and suffering, and most of it is ours to carry."

Zephyr pulled me into his shadows and dropped me on my balcony before I had time to ask another question, before I could tell him not to kill innocents, before I could remind him that I was already destined to die in Elphame. I wondered if his hunt played a role in my fate. If he did not go, would my fate change and I'd be stuck forever in Elphame, either on the run or locked in a prison being groomed into a nightmare?

The roof above my bedroom looked like a mountain had blown apart, sending its rocks landing in one place. Gargoyles of all sizes perched in their slumber—more than I could count. It didn't frighten me to see them, but it also did nothing to calm my nerves. I had one day left.

"I told you they were pests," Nix called out from my bedroom door.

I spun with an ear-to-ear smile, the kind of happiness that sprung from the soul. "Nix."

"Do you mind if I come in?" he asked, still nervous about me and my grief. He stood on the hall side of my door, waiting for an invitation.

I ducked into my room and knelt at the foot of my bed. I opened my arms for him. "Well, don't just stand there. Come here."

Nix jumped into my arms and buried his face in my hair. I had so many things to say, but tears were all that mustered their way out. We sat like that until I felt all my pieces come back together. I hadn't realized until now, with Nix gone, that a big part of me was missing.

"I'm so sorry, Nix. You were never a problem. I was. I'm sorry." I cried into his little body, not ever wanting to let go. "Don't leave me again."

He squirmed and pulled back, sitting in the crook of my arm. "I had to take Elswyth—" he started, but my hard look of knowing the truth stopped him. "I felt like a reminder. I lied to you so much and played a role in your suffering. I thought, if I left, you'd heal, then maybe I could come back and apologize. I don't know. I just wanted you to get better, whatever the cost."

"I wasn't a good friend to you, Nix."

"Don't say that. You've been my closest friend for as long as I can remember."

I shook my head. "No. Maybe once I was. But the pain, the memories… I was looking for someone to blame. I was looking for a reason. But it wasn't your fault any more than it was my own. You did your best in the situation you were in. You were given a task, and I can't thank you enough for fulfilling it. I love you, Nix, and I would have died without you so many times. You have always been my friend. You've faced death with me, such horrors, and never once did you leave my side to save yourself. I didn't even think you'd need help after the Golden Court. Are you okay?"

He smiled and snuggled back in. "It was hard. It still is. But everything feels a little lighter now that I'm here."

"How is Elswyth?" I asked.

Nix shrugged. "She's numb, like the rest of us. She's lived a hard life, Perdi. And now, she's free. There's a lot of healing to be done."

"Did you meet her soon-to-be husband?"

"No, I caught wind of war and returned."

"You came back for war?" I laughed.

He popped up with a laugh. "You can't be the only one to have the fun."

"I wouldn't call it fun," I muttered. As happy as I was to see him, I'd be leaving him, too. I felt instantly sad once again.

"I came back for you, Perdi. I know what will happen at the Gate," he whispered. "You won't be alone in the end. I'll be there, and I'll make sure you are brought home. I swear on my life, I won't leave you there for the birds. I will bring you home, where you belong."

My eyes watered. "You know?"

He nodded. "It will take all you are to stop this. I'm not a fool. And I wouldn't have you face it alone."

I smiled through my tears. "I'm so sorry, Nix."

"Don't. I will not grieve you yet—and neither will you. Live every moment, Perdi. It's all we have, our moments of happiness."

I sniffled and cleaned my face of tears. "You're right."

"I've heard you've been training with Zephyr. How's that been going?" He changed the topic, and I let him.

I shrugged. "As good as one could imagine training with a"—I paused—"Aos Si would be."

"A *what*?" Nix asked, and I looked away. "Oh, that. Yeah, I know that, too. Remember, I'm small, and people never think to look down when they're telling their secrets."

I stared at him for a long moment to see if he truly knew. Nix mimicked eating the air, and I laughed. I raised my eyebrows, didn't confirm or deny, but didn't risk saying it out loud.

"I won't say the words out loud, either. I just got here. I'd hate to have to leave so soon again, unwillingly," Nix answered. He looked around my room, still destroyed. "I love what you've done with the place. It's very open concept and minimalist."

"I had a bit of a fire." I blushed.

"Uh-huh." He smiled and froze, turning to the balcony. "He's coming."

"Who?" I asked. "Zephyr?"

"No, worse…Solas." Nix smiled. "Yes, I've already heard about you both – and your room smells of him."

I felt the heat tickle my neck. "It just happened."

"I'm not judging you, Perdi." Nix kissed my nose. "He's almost died for you countless times. If you can't love the man who will die for you, who can you love?"

"I didn't say I loved him," I answered.

"Uh-huh," Nix answered and jumped off my legs and out of the door as I moved to the balcony.

"I'm glad you're back, Nix," I called from outside.

"Are you ready?" Solas landed beside me, and I screamed.

"Ready? For what?" I asked, clutching my pounding heart.

"For me to show you what we're fighting for," he answered and grabbed my waist. I was off the ground, in his arms, wrapped in wind and black smoke. One moment I stood on my balcony, looking up at the war that waited, nested on the roof. The next, I stood behind the mountains, in his court, the Court of Shadows, the most feared place in Elphame. Every terrifying story ended in this court, and it was beautiful. Solas hadn't brought me here until now, when I needed to see it most.

The city was incredible. Black stone, dark granite, rose from the earth and formed buildings and shops and houses and halls. The Sluagh caves overlooked every inch of a land Solas had become a monster to protect. We stood in a bowl, held in the mountains, trees towered above, and on every tip stood the Sluagh, ready and waiting to defend the court. The streets were lined with tiny black stones, glittering like stars. So many Fae bustled about, and children of all sizes filled the streets with laughter. It reminded me of Whitwick, from the smells to the sounds. Everything moved together, fit together, as if one single piece missing would be noticed.

"Why on earth would you not choose to live here?" I asked. "It's beautiful."

"War, little Crow. If I lived here, they'd always come for me here. I won't bring that to my people," he answered, and it made perfect sense. "And, could you imagine the Sluagh traipsing down these streets? The bills for damage alone would break my treasury—not to mention those they'd trample would be less than understanding."

Solas held out his elbow, and I slipped my arm into his. He walked me through the streets, pointing out where he grew up, where he and Zephyr had met, where he'd broken his arm as a child fighting and where Zephyr had broken his arm again the day they'd met. Every block had a memory attached—some were fond, and some made him shudder and shake the memory away before he felt the pain of it fully. We both passed the sweet shop, knowing I'd prefer never to taste candy again. The book shop grabbed my full attention. I roamed the isles while Solas spoke with the gentleman at the counter, like they had been close friends. I found a book then frowned.

"Is something wrong?" Solas stepped to my side.

"Yes, I don't actually have any money." I started to laugh. "Do Fae use money?"

"Yes, we have money." He pulled me into his front. "Don't worry. You can pay me back later, in favors and flesh."

I shoved him off and felt my cheeks heat. "You're awful."

Solas put the charge for the book on his account. He teased me out in the streets, pinching my rear as I swatted him and laughed. He finally relented and pulled me under his arm. We dined in the park and drank wine under the stars on a balcony overlooking the city. It was everything I wanted my last night in Elphame to be. I thought it would hurt more, knowing I'd leave, but it felt right. In my bones, it felt like an end that needed to happen, the end to what could be a new beginning for mortals and Fae alike. I didn't mind being the Crow tonight, the sacrifice for all.

"It's peaceful here. I don't want to leave," I finally said, breaking up a comfortable silence with an uncomfortable topic.

"Don't. You don't have to leave here or the manor. Tomorrow is your choice. I won't force it on you," he replied. "If you don't want to leave, stay."

"I have to go."

His face fell slightly. Disappointed. "I don't want you to."

"I know, but I also don't want there to ever be another Crow. I want to be the last."

"You asked once what I feared. This is it, Perdi. I fear losing all this—my people, my friends, those I love...you."

I didn't bother feeding him lies or comforts, but the truth was too difficult to say out loud. I cupped his face and kissed him as deeply as I could. I wanted to taste him to his core. I wanted to remember what he felt like. I needed to feel every fiber of his being. I needed to drink him down because I'd never get the chance again. I wanted to leave him with a piece of me, a part of goodness, to force him to hold on once I was gone. A tether in the storm that would be coming and would crush him. He would feel as I once had, alone and completely heartbroken.

My breath caught in my throat as his teeth nipped at my neck. We made love under the stars, in a land made of nightmares, and it was a perfect end.

"Whatever happens tomorrow, know that this was the best night of my life," I whispered into his chest and drifted to sleep with the sound of his beating heart under my hand.

Chapter Eleven

The sun rose over the Dark Courts, and with it came my last day. I started the day surrounded by those I cared for deeply, and those I had learned had a place in my heart. And in those moments, I felt the weight of every decision I had ever made—from the moment I'd met Faolan to setting the darkness free upon Elphame. They rested on my shoulders, heavier now than when I had first made them. Every act and turn and choice had led me to the conclusion of my short life.

Before I left my bedroom, I placed the book of poetry I had purchased on my bed, with a final goodbye to Solas.

Know deep in your heart how very deep you are in mine.

You deserve so much more than what I'm leaving you with.

Find peace.

I love you,

Little Crow.

I thought I'd have more regrets when I came to the end of my life, but I didn't, not really. If I had to do it all over, I wouldn't change the path, only the strength I found along the way. To change anything, I suppose, would have taken me away from this moment. And as much as I didn't want to die here, I also didn't want hundreds of Crows to die in my place. I had to be here. I had to do this. Those who had come before me had carved my path. They had done all they could to make the last leg of my journey as painless as possible. But no greatness ever came without pain. No act worthy of notice from the Gods ever came without the bleeding of souls. I would be the sacrifice they had been waiting for. If I wasn't willing to lose what I held dear, my life, for what I wanted, all I wanted would be sacrificed instead.

I was only a child when I'd learned what true sacrifice was, when my mother gave her life for who she was. I had thought I'd never feel that kind of pain again. Until Elphame, I had no idea what sacrifice could be. Now, as I stood on the precipice of war, I was finally a willing tithe to the Gods and Goddesses. It both scared and settled me.

The Aos Si army, the Sluagh, gargoyles and beasts had spent the night moving the last of the families out of the Court of Less and into the protected lands of the Sluagh. Those from the Seelie and Unseelie Courts who came to the Dark borders seeking sanctuary were granted a safe place to hide. No one was turned away. War was ugly, but it didn't need to be cruel to those who didn't stand between each army.

The Golden King, Theofanis, burned the lands between his court and us, leaving the charred remains as a reminder that war didn't care if you were innocent.

Those who stood against him were left to die on the road to the Courtless. Theofanis and his armies stood between the Gate and me. Nothing was left but smoke and death. I was wrong about Theofanis. He was not like his father. He was worse. But war made everyone worse. It twisted us and pushed us to do the unthinkable. To live, to protect those we love, we burned everything that stood between us and that which we cherished.

Solas stood at the front, his army behind us. I could smell the blood before I saw the bodies. Ahead of us, the ground was littered with pieces, limbs and flesh left behind by Theofanis. As far as my eyes could see, it was bloody and brutal. It was not a war that left those bodies, but a message from Theofanis, a warning. Theofanis chose his weapon wisely—fear. But he was young and hadn't seen the true horrors that followed behind Solas. He hadn't seen the terrors hiding from sight.

I moved to Solas' side and looked out as Theofanis' army grew in numbers as they spread across the field. It looked like a storm rolling in. The ground thundered under my feet as they moved. I looked at Solas, and he was smiling. He wasn't afraid. His entire life, hundreds of years, boiled down to this one moment, this tick in time. His fate had finally come. His courage radiated out to his people. And as the army grew under our close watch, not a single one of Solas' people flinched. They, like Solas, grinned in anticipation. The Dark Courts were bred for war. This was what they did. It was who they were. They were born and bred in the bellies of beasts.

"Are you ready?" I asked him.

"I always am, little Crow."

"You seem calm."

"War doesn't scare me. I was born into this world with a sword in my hands." He closed his eyes and sighed. "I'm not afraid of death. I'm scared to lose those I'd leave behind. I'm scared to never see those I love again."

It took me several tries to speak again. My heart caught in my throat. "Will you die down there?"

"I don't believe so, no."

"How comforting." I smirked.

"There are no guarantees, especially not in war." He turned to face me. "If I were to fall, run. If I'm dead, Zephyr likely will be, too. Go with the Sluagh. They'll hide you. They will grant you and Nix safe passage. If you don't, you'll be hunted down with the full force of every court."

"What about the Gate?"

"You'd never make it. You'd die before you got there," he answered. "Promise me, Perdi, that you'll run."

I nodded.

"Say the words. If I'm dead, if Zephyr is dead, you'll run. Do *not* go back to the mortal world. They won't be safe if we are gone. We are the only ones who have stood between Elphame and the mortal realm."

"I promise. If you both fall, I'll run," I agreed. "Promise me, you'll do everything you can to survive. No matter what happens, you'll keep living."

He pulled me in for a tight hug. "I promise."

He didn't know what he was promising me. It had nothing to do with battle and everything to do with his will to live when he realized I wouldn't come back out from the Gate. He kissed my forehead, pausing like he was memorizing what I looked like, and was gone. Like that, a cloud of mist trailing the earth, he was gone to his men.

"I love you," I whispered to him, but he'd disappeared, not having heard it.

Zephyr stepped up to my side and squeezed my shoulder. "He loves you."

"I needed him to hear it, once." I looked up at Zephyr. "I'm not going to leave the Gate alive."

"I know," he answered but kept his eyes forward, watching, waiting for his turn to strike. "I've always known."

"How?"

"From the moment I knew you'd come, I've known we'd end up here. Just as I know you will walk into the mists of the Gate and will die there for us all," he answered. "And now, I can feel it in your pearl—a sadness that only the deepest of sacrifices can bring."

"When I die, can you release my pearl so I'm not stuck here?" I asked.

"Of course."

"Zeph, bring my body home. Don't leave me in there to rot. Bring me home, please?" I whispered and breathed through the threat of tears. I would not cry on this field and willed my tears back through blinks and sheer force. Elphame had gotten enough of my tears already.

Zephyr squeezed my arm and nodded. "I'm honored to have known you, Perdita Darkmore, Soul-Eater, little Crow. Your sacrifice will forever be remembered, and not a day will go by where I won't curse the Gods with your name."

"Solas will need you. Don't leave him."

"It is time to fly, little Crow."

The world around me exploded in magick and power, rolling tendrils of darkness, shadows that ate all in their path and the rumble of thousands of bodies closing the gap between the Seelie and Unseelie. The clash of sword against shield and screams of pain filled the crisp morning air. I looked above as the Sluagh fought against creatures on wings, painting the sky in red. Beasts climbed through the earth and ate battalions of men on both sides. The trees bled with nymphs of all shapes and terrifying sizes. Men who tried to cross the river drowned before their hair was wet. I watched the dark court eat the light and everything that stood in its way.

My heart broke in sadness.

But this was war.

My stomach rolled at the carnage.

War was nothing more than the dance of the dead.

My eyes watered at the sounds of blood and bones.

But war was never meant as an act of kindness.

I scanned the masses, watching and waiting. Solas cut through swathes of men as if they were butter. Wave after wave tried and failed to take Solas from this world. It almost pained me to think that even in war, he was beautiful and graceful. But he was. If terror could ever look elegant and stunning while taking a life, that was Solas. It was a dance he had mastered over decades of death. His entire body moved as one, yet every part of him moved differently. It was as though he already knew the movement of the other before they did, and he struck them down before they knew well enough that they were already dead the moment they woke up this morning.

On the other side of the field was Zephyr. Where Solas was liquid grace, Zephyr was a raging fire. Men fell, and Zephyr climbed over their bodies as if they were ground and beneath his notice. Once they went down, they were of no more consequence. And when the armies moved toward Solas, Zephyr's men moved to cut them in half, dwindling the numbers against Solas. I knew after just minutes of watching that Zephyr had ordered his men to protect Solas before himself. And when groups came for Zephyr, Solas' rage billowed from his soul, cutting them down before they could strike against his most loyal friend.

Zephyr had once said he'd give anything to have the kind of loyalty Nix gave me, someone who would die for him. But Zephyr did, even if he didn't know it. Solas would give his life, his very soul, to save Zephyr. They each would. I felt calm with that knowledge.

"It's uglier down there." Nix hopped onto my shoulder. He would be with me until the end. "From here, you can almost pretend. But once you step onto that field, the curtain comes up, and you can smell the colors you can only see from here. Each scream can be felt in your soul. Time will move differently down there. Every minute will feel longer. Every inch feels like fifty yards to cross. You will fight for everything. Every breath, step, inch, second will feel impossible to gain."

"How many wars have you fought?" I asked him. I had never thought to ask before.

"Until I went to the mortal realm, every single war this cursed place has waged. I've lost count. No one is safe from war here. You're either fighting in it, dying in it or suffering because of it." He shivered as old memories came back. "I may be small, but I've never lost."

"This is my first, and I can't lose."

"Are you ready for it?" he asked. "Unlike every other war fought, we are fighting to get to the Gate, that is all. There is no other task. This battle will be over within a couple of hours, not days or weeks. But for you, it'll feel like weeks."

I nodded and drank the power from the air. I would need it all when I got to the Gate. I closed my eyes and felt every soul who dropped from a sword or magick, felt every wound from battle. I ate the fear and pain and remorse. Not once did I feel regret from Solas or his people as my Malice flowed through the field. They fought, knowing what they were fighting for, the future of their people and a chance for their families and children to be free and safe. They fought for me and were willing to die to give me a chance. They, like me, would give anything for the Gate to close, to no longer watch children dragged into Elphame. They, like Solas, hated the Taking.

At my back, twenty Aos Si stepped out of the darkness. Zephyr had saved the best of his men for me. They dressed as if the very night had wrapped them in armor and weapons. My eyes found Zephyr, and he nodded. I looked to Solas, and even from here, I saw him smile. The clouds above opened, and pools of darkness fell to the earth. The Sluagh. I felt the rumble from every corner of the Court of Less. Everyone would fight, man and beast, and we saved the worst we had for last.

"I'm ready." I finally spoke.

"To war, we go," Nix called out.

This was it. I ran toward certain death and didn't stop. My little creature joined the run, flying at my side, her teeth bared to the world, already covered in the blood of the unfortunate soldier who'd dismissed her as a warrior. Behind, hundreds of her brethren followed. They covered the enemy in waves, picking them clean of their meat. The screams were, as Nix had warned me, felt deep in my soul and down to my toes. Nix jumped from shoulder to shoulder and tore at their necks, not waiting for them to bleed out before moving on to the next.

I ducked and jumped and skidded across blood and remains. A run that should have taken me twenty minutes felt like days had already gone by. Every second was stretched out to impossible lengths. I knew where I had to go but found the trip unbearably long with mountains to climb between here and the Gate. Although I had been told, it was always different when you actually lived it. I had run across the entirety of Elphame, being chased by every creature of this realm, yet that run felt like I had done it in half the time it had taken for me to move a few feet on this field. It was as if everything was happening too fast and my movements too slow.

The world slipped, and I went forward under the weight of another. Before I could scream, the man on top of me let out his own. I struggled from under him and flipped to face the sky. A soldier was fighting Nix, who was too slippery with blood to be held long enough for death to come. The temptation to suck his soul dry was tempting, but it was a last resort. I pulled my knife and pressed it under his chin. I didn't wait for him to drop Nix. I shoved it in and twisted. The warmth of his blood was almost relieving against the cold stickiness that already covered my hands.

Zephyr pulled the man from my body. "It's not nap time yet, little Crow. Get moving."

I nodded and swallowed my urge to vomit. I had killed before. I'd killed the Golden King with this very knife. This was no more or less horrifying. Taking a life, even in war, would stain the last few minutes of my life. I was not born of war. But I had learned fast enough that Elphame didn't care where I was born or why. War still came.

"Move!" Zephyr pulled me to my feet.

"Solas?" I asked. My heart was now in my throat. "Am I running to the Gate? Or am I running away?"

"He's alive. The Gate… Get to the Gate."

Zephyr cleaned swathes of soldiers from my path and barked orders at the others to fall in line behind Solas. But they wouldn't be there to fight beside him. It was time, and Solas would need to be held back. The only ones strong enough to contain him were the Aos Si and Zephyr. The Sluagh, although they answered to Solas, wouldn't help him with this. They, like everyone else, wanted the Gate closed and knew the cost. I glanced at Solas, who was making his way to me, as I reached the shimmering wall that held the Gate inside.

"Goodbye," I whispered.

Zephyr moved to stand between Solas and me. "I am privileged to be written in the books with you, the Crow who burned the world for all of our freedoms." He tilted his head, a salute, and left me to a destiny written long before the Gate was formed.

I stepped to the shimmering wall that split the worlds and breathed in the scent that rolled through from home. I looked back at Solas, not to remember him in battle, but to remember why I was doing this. Eventually, this would mean there'd be no more reason for war. On this day, what each of us gave on the field, would mean something. When Solas saw Zephyr, he realized in that heartbreaking moment what my fate would be, what sacrifice I would become. A Crow is not a sacrifice unless she dies for her realm. The battle, still going, raged around him. He cleared his path, like water can clear villages off the map. But it wouldn't matter because Zephyr could not be moved—not by Solas, not by the entire war.

He ran faster, screaming my name. "Wait! No! Perdi, *no*!"

"I love you," I answered and motioned for Zephyr.

Zephyr ran to Solas and tackled him, lifting him off the ground and slamming him down. Solas bucked and screamed, but no magick or power would pull Zephyr from him. He commanded and ordered, but not even the Gods could control a Soul-Eater. Zephyr covered them both in his shadows, a brick wall of darkness to hold Solas in. I looked at Nix, standing mere yards from me, and smiled. His face crumpled, but he still nodded. No matter what the Gate threw at me today, it would never be as painful as knowingly leaving behind those I loved.

I stepped into the fog, the same inky mist that had Taken me from my home, from my people. Once, I had been terrified. Now, I stepped in and closed my eyes. I stood straight and allowed myself to take it all in. I had crossed the threshold. I had made it to the Gate. I was both in here and out there…two worlds. I stood inside the white mist, but beyond the wisps of power, I could see Elphame. It was like looking through water. Beyond the haze of the Gate, the war raged on. Men lived and died for this moment. Solas was kneeling on the ground, still screaming my name. Zephyr and his men circled him and fought off every man who approached. Solas begged for my return. He would find a different way. But there were no other ways. There was only this. Hearing him beg me broke my heart. He once told me that I would learn true pain in Elphame. Today, right now, the lesson had been learned. I turned from Solas and the pain in his voice.

Ahead, two trees and a single black gate—the Gate we all suffered for, and oh, did we suffer. A rift between the fabrics of our realms had cursed both worlds equally. The ground crunched with each step I took toward the Gate. The white mist darkened the closer I got to my fate. It felt like walking through thick water. Each step took more and more effort. My heart dragged behind me, holding on to Solas screaming my name, begging me to return to him, telling me he'd rather fight a million wars. The harder I tried to silence that hurt, that tug within me, the thicker the air grew around me.

The Gate swung open with a cry, its hinges rusted with time. Through the Gate, a young woman staggered, her eyes wide with fear and darting wildly. The girl had hair like her mother and like her mother's mother. Her nightgown was stained in blood. Her cheeks streaked from tears. It was like looking in a mirror at myself the day I came through the Gate, terrified but not yet stained and broken.

"Who are you?" I asked.

"Aoife," she answered. She reached out to me. "Trust no one."

I smiled at my greatest of grandmothers. "You can trust Solas."

She stared at me for a moment and nodded. She walked through the mist and was gone, gone to a time that had passed long ago. I wasn't alone in the fog. Hundreds of Crows before me lingered as memories. I could feel them. They were gone but would always be a part of Elphame, a part of me, a part of what I was doing. Together, we all gave ourselves to the Gate, in one way or another.

Go back.

Echoed around me from all sides.

You're not welcome here, little Crow.

"No," I answered plainly.

Give me back that which you took, and I will allow you to live.

"No," I answered again. I would not bargain with the very thing that helped kill my people. "You gave it freely."

You took it.

"You didn't stop me. The power was mine, gifted from generations of Darkmore witches before. It was left here for me to take, for this very moment."

I know why you've come.

"Then you know I cannot turn back now."

You will die here.

"I know."

I cannot allow this.

"And I cannot allow this to continue."

You will try, and you will fail. She will not allow this.

I hesitated for a blink of an eye. Who was *she,* and what would *she* not allow?

She, the opener of the Gate.

She, the bringer of Blood and Bones.

"*She* is not here to stop me," I answered. "*She* can fight for my blood and bones once I'm dead."

You're a foolish child.

You bring damnation.

"I bring *your* damnation."

The Gate cannot be destroyed.

"But I can close it, and you can rust for all of eternity."

You will fail.

I found myself smiling. "I've heard that song before, yet here I am."

You will die.

"We all die. This is as good as any reason to die."

I have secrets you want, truths you seek.

I can let you go home and never come back.

"I am home."

The air grew thin and cold. Frost coated my skin. My teeth chattered, and I fell to my knees, dizzy as if the air were being sucked from my lungs. My vision danced with stars as I starved for one more breath. I pulled the knife from my sheath and sliced my shaking hand. I let the blood pour from my wound and soak the ground, guided by memory not my own. I could hear my mother and her mother and her mother's mother whispering around me. The fog held memories of those long forgotten, and now they were mine.

With knot one, the spell has begun.
With knot two, my heart is true.
With knot three, so mote it be.
With knot four, the Gate is no more.
With knot five, our people shall thrive.
With knot six, the Gate can never be fixed.
With knot seven, this spell will not lessen.
With knot eight, this spell is our fate.
With a knot of nine, the cost is mine.
So mote it be.

I cried out as the power, the magick, my Malice, burst through me and filled the mist. Every voice who had stepped through the Gate screamed from my bones. The power blasted through the vapor and threw me through the air into a crumpled heap. Through the whiteness, I could see my Malice snake across the frosted ground, unbothered by the cold. Screaming filled my ears until I realized the screams came from my own mouth.

The Gate slammed shut, and I felt it in my marrow. With the final beats of my heart, the spell would seal. Now all that was left was the cost for me to pay. I relaxed in the cold seeping into my body. On my back, I smiled my last smile as the cold touch of my payment rushed in. It was worth it. Even as the little air I had left was slowly ripped and snatched from my lungs by talons I couldn't see, I would be left with no scars of regret. Very few deaths are glorious, and even fewer that I'd been present for had been worth watching. But mine? I wasn't disappointed in a single moment of it. It *was* glorious. It was everything I thought it would be and more.

"I win." I exhaled a long and shaking breath.

I'd played their games. I'd danced to their music. I'd drunk their wine. And I'd left my blood on their floors. But I broke their backs. I ruined their kingdoms. I painted their walls with their failures. I was the last, the very last Crow, and for that, I was grateful and willing to pay the cost. There would never be another to be lashed, tortured or beaten. There would never be another Crow stolen from their home and families. When babies were birthed, there would be no more prayers that their child would be spared Elphame. They would finally celebrate lives, knowing they wouldn't become a sacrifice to a realm of no mercy. This moment, as broken as I was, as empty as I felt, was worth becoming a Crow. Every night I had spent here, wishing I was home, I'd do it again, three times over, to be at this moment again.

At eighteen, I had lived countless lives in the span of a year, and now the struggle was over. I closed my eyes. I could die knowing I gave everything. My fragile, half-human heart finally stopped its fight. I had made it to the end, and I had saved every soul I could along the way. With my death, I saved them all.

My name is Perdita Darkmore.

I saved them all.

I am the last Crow.

And I died for these wings.

* * * *

I was fated to die in Elphame. And I did, painfully and freely. But death isn't always as fast as living can be. Sometimes life is short and fleeting. Whereas death takes his time and draws it out until he, himself, is ready to leave the table. He was a fickle creature and came and went as he pleased on a clock no one could see.

The pain that once burned my flesh like a fire had faded away into the icy numbness that had glazed my body in a thick blanket. Black edged my vision until the only thing I could hear was the final beats of my pulse, hard and heavy and without desire for more. My breath came in ragged, shallow gasps, unwilling to let go, but it gave me nothing. Seconds or hours or days, I lay there, alone and cold…and waiting. There was no pain left, just waiting. As soon as my pulse stopped, I'd wait for death, only for it to thump once again.

I wondered, for a moment, if this was how it was for all people. Did the time between life and death pass as slowly, giving them time to contemplate their lives? Was this how life had flashed before people's eyes? Or was this part of my payment, to suffer until the bitter end? I doubted I was that special.

Noise cut through the darkness and nudged at the parts of me still waiting on death. Voices from those who still wanted to save me, in vain. Even if I had wanted to, if I could have left the mist, I could never escape payment. I could never hide from a debt attached to my very soul. But I didn't want to, not really. If I could have crawled through the mist, I wouldn't have. It was better this way—better I go without having to see the pain of my loss on the faces of those I loved. I didn't want the last things I saw to be despair and suffering in a world that had taken everything from me and given so little in return. This way, in the mist, I could leave all of it behind. I would fade into the haze of the Gate, where this started and where it would end.

"Breathe, Perdi!" Solas screamed my name, but I was still in the mist, too far away to tell him to let me go, to say goodbye, to remind him once again how deeply he was loved. I faded again.

"Perdi." Nix's voice pulled me back up from the fog. "Fight. You have to fight this time. Don't let it take you."

I had no fight left in me. I had given it all for this moment. My limbs were as heavy as my heart, and my soul had already given up, spent on ending the Taking.

"Please, don't leave me. You're all I've got." I could taste Nix's tears in the back of my throat, and every memory of us flooded my mind, chasing away the darkness settling in.

I remembered first meeting him, slowly coaxing him out of hiding, and finally granting him my backyard and my protection. He swore his allegiance to me, as I did to him. They were innocent words, said by a child without understanding the weight of their meaning. But even then, I had meant them and still did. I protected him against all who came, and he, in turn, gave everything for me.

"Nix," I whispered wordlessly, no air to carry my voice.

My body jerked against the ground. Was this what death felt like? Heart-wrenching pain and nothing more? I tried to lift my arms, but each movement sent searing pain through my chest. My heart felt like it was going to explode, gripped in a vise I couldn't see or break free from. The agony was immense, too great to fight through. The cost was upon me, and I could do not a thing to stop it. It was everything. It was consuming. It pushed and pulled at every inch of my body, like birds picking at a carcass.

"It's not your time," Nix cried.

"Help," I finally muttered through gritted teeth.

I focused on the only thing I knew. I called the darkness. I called the shadows as I had so many times before. I called on them as I had in the dungeon when I had been scared and alone and dying of infection. Little by little, I could feel the warmth of the shadows pressing down on me. With them came air, and I gulped it down.

"Please." I struggled to move but was utterly still. "Help."

In the darkness, Zephyr knelt beside me. Gone was the blood of battle. Gone was the war that lined his face. He had lost his weapons and armor. He crossed his legs and sat beside me, dressed in black and the kind of kindness that only I ever found in his dark blue eyes. Where everyone else saw him as a Soul-Eater, I saw the depth of his love and loyalty. Like Solas, who hid behind a mask, Zephyr wasn't as scary once you loved him.

"What did you take from the Gate, little Crow, to cause it this much anger? You are broken."

"What is mine to have. What was left behind for me," I replied.

"Not all power is for the taking."

"It is when you're a Soul-Eater," I answered. "Help me."

"Do you want to live? Knowing you'll be hunted for who you are?"

"Yes."

Zephyr rolled my pearl in his palm. I felt his touch as if I were the one in his hand. "It is a life I'd wish on no one, little Crow. It is a path that will be rife with heartache."

"I'm not ready to go."

"We are never ready to go when our time comes."

"It's not my time. Not yet."

"We do not decide when our time comes. We do not have power over fate. She is alone in her decisions."

I tried to shake my head but was lifeless in my movements. "*I* decide my fate, Zeph."

"Only a Soul-Eater can come back with the souls eaten from another. It is the very reason why kings take us. It is why armies killed us twice and scattered our ashes for good measure. We can walk the in-between and choose those who live and those who die. We take life, and we can give life back. But know this, Perdi. We will be hunted for this. Are you willing to die twice?"

"Yes." One word was the only answer I could muster before the pain came and took everything else from me.

"You know this will only bring you more pain, more suffering. But you can stop it. I could take all your pain away, and you would move on to the next life, free of this all. I would carry your body to your final resting place and not a day would go by when you weren't at peace."

I tried to shake my head and failed. My limbs didn't feel like my own anymore. "I know."

"No, you don't. You will always be a little Crow. You're made only to suffer, and there will be so much of it that you'll curse me for this day. You'll be forced to fight for each and every step. If you live, you'll live the life I never wanted for you. You'll live the life of a Soul-Eater and will pay for it dearly. You'll never be free, not ever."

"I...decide..." I groaned. "How do...?"

"How do I know? Because your fate is bound to mine, and I've never had a single day of peace. Nothing has ever come easy to me, not even you. If you choose this, you are choosing to walk the same painful path I have and still do. You're not going to live. You're just choosing to die on a different day—and every day in between will be a fight for the next."

I wondered how badly I'd regret this decision.

"That's for you to decide when you come to your last page. But I suspect it'll hurt far too much for there to be any room for regret."

"Please."

"Foolish. Little. Crow."

"Soul-Eater," I muttered back.

"Be thankful for that." He pressed his palm into my chest. "This is going to be unlike any pain you've ever felt before."

"Everything hurts in—" My words cut off. The moment he touched my heart, my body jerked as if every lightning bolt ever to have landed had struck only me.

The world sped up around me. Between the grip of death I was being pulled from and the reality I was being shoved back into, it felt like being skinned alive and rolled in salt. It was beyond agony. This feeling would become a new measurement for pain. The lashes in the Golden Court had nothing on this. I felt it from the inside out—screaming, death, war, pain and my ribs cracking under a force I didn't understand. Screeches from Sluagh pierced my ears and left them ringing. I felt my body jerk and twist and pull in every direction. High-pitched cries rattled against my bones.

"Aoife, you lied! You said she'd come back to me. You swore she'd live. You promised me!" Solas screamed into the night. He held my limp, bloodied and broken body against his chest. His tears fell from his eyes and rolled down my cheeks. "I love you, Perdita Darkmore. You can't leave me. I just found you. Come back, please, my little Crow."

I swam up from the dark wasteland I had rested in, readying for death. I clawed my way back to life, back to Solas, to his voice, back to my home. I struggled against the pull to rest, to give in, to let fate make the decision for me. Soupy fog clung to me, but I didn't stop fighting. It felt like months had passed, and every step forward was a marathon. I kicked and swam for the surface where my life waited for me. As the darkness faded, I clung to the light and let it bring me to the top, where I gasped for my first pure breath since I had stepped into the Gate.

"Stop calling me that."

He jerked and dropped me to the ground. He stared at me for a short moment. Confusion played over his blood-stained face. "Perdi?"

I squinted against the brilliance of the sun and smiled, calling him by his nickname. "*Soulless.*"

He scrambled to pick me back up. He hugged me tightly against him. "I thought you were gone. I prayed for you to come back." He breathed me in and shuddered. "You're whole again. I thought… God, I love you."

"I love you, too." I rolled my head to see Zephyr standing, back in his leathers, covered in the blood of war. "Took you long enough."

Zephyr shook his head. "A simple 'thank you' works."

"Thank you," I finally said and closed my eyes. "I never want to do that again."

"Then you should not have chosen to live." Zephyr's words were only for me.

Dead or alive, I still paid painfully for my Malice. Only now Solas ate what he could and kept my heart beating. I wasn't alone. I didn't have to do this on my own. Those I loved, who loved me in return, were with me and did what they could to love me as I suffered for them all.

Chapter Twelve

The war ended the moment I closed the Gate. The force of magick that poured from the Gate, wild and free, ate those not smart enough to run, those not under the protection of the Dark Courts. Hundreds died in the war, but not a single person from our lands had backed down or given in. The Dark Court had stood firm. Mothers took up weapons, stones and swords and stood firm at the edge of their lands, ready to fight for the lives of their children, ready to fight for the children of the Seelie and Unseelie who had sought shelter. They, those who were considered the weakest in the eyes of our enemies, fought against evil with mere stones and bravery, unlike anything the Golden Court had seen before. They had come to these lands believing we were weak. They had no idea how utterly powerful a mother protecting a child could be, and those who tempted fate died swiftly and without remorse.

War wasn't ugly in places where the people stood together against evil and tyranny. Those who had once played victim to the games of the more powerful stood shoulder to shoulder around those who could no longer stand or fight. Prisoners who still bore the bruises upon their bodies fought tooth and nail to ensure their people would not be taken to dungeons again. Stragglers who managed to get past Solas and his army were hunted like the dogs they were by the women who once had begged the dogs for the pain to stop. When caught, there had been no amount of pleading that could keep back what they had earned.

The Gate was closed, and the mortals who were now trapped in Elphame were found and offered sanctuary. Without help, without protection, they'd fall prey to the powerful. The weak were always victims of the strong in both the mortal and Fae realms. The Fae outside, in the mortal realm, either wanted to be there or deserved to be cut off from Elphame, for they were only in the mortal lands to bring anarchy and madness to the people. Now they would suffer that same fate. They'd slowly wither and starve of Fae magick. Having seen what the brink of madness could do to another, I knew it was a fate worse than death.

I had spent days in bed, sleeping, barely waking for food or drink. A deep sleep had sucked me under on the battlefield, surrounded by those who had fought and died to close that Gate. Zephyr had brought me home, as he had promised. Each time I woke, Nix was there, on my pillow. When a visitor came, they left empty-handed. Nix chanced no one and nothing. Until I was strong enough to protect myself, he, my little friend, would protect me. I woke to him and his sword, trying to fight off Zephyr. Nix won, not because Zephyr was stronger, but because Nix deserved his right to protect his only living family member. Solas was the only one Nix didn't bar and the only one he trusted to watch over me in his absence.

But Nix couldn't keep the shadows at bay, not wholly. You can't stop what you can't grab. And when Nix couldn't fight them, he stayed seated on my legs, fighting to hold me in a world the shadows weren't tethered to. If they wanted to take me, they were taking him with them, and they did. They held me and healed me. They brought me energy and rebuilt the pieces of my soul that I scuffed off in the Gate. Soon, Nix didn't mind them. He understood why they were coming.

While asleep, Solas had replaced all my broken furniture. Knowing I was locked in Elphame for eternity, Solas carved out a space for me. When I finally woke, I didn't know how I felt about it. I didn't know how I felt about anything. I was happy to be alive, but so many had paid dearly for it. It was a debt I'd carry with me forever.

"The fog thickened, and Zephyr couldn't feel you anymore. I tried to get in, to get to you, but I couldn't pass. It was a wall, and nothing I did could break it." Solas spoke quietly, stroking my back. As hard as he tried, I could still hear the hint of fear and tears in his voice. "I tried to force Zephyr to go in and get you, but he wouldn't. He wouldn't force you to come back. I tried everything to make him save you, but he kept telling me he wouldn't fate you with a painful path unless you asked for it."

"I'm so sorry." My heart broke for him and the fear and loss he had felt.

"When I thought all hope was lost, I heard the screeches from the sky. On the shoulders of the Sluagh,

Nix and Orrian stood, leading a dozen into the fog. Nix and your little creature dragged you from the Gate to my waiting hands."

"How did the Sluagh get in, but you couldn't?" I asked.

"They didn't come back out, Perdi. They breached a space big enough for only Nix and Orrian to get in and out, to bring you back."

I touched his face gently and closed my eyes. "Thank you," I said to those who gave and gave for me to live. "I'm so sorry for your losses, Solas."

"They gave willingly, Perdi, and I will not forget. This court will never forget their sacrifice. Both Zephyr and I have spent time with the families of the fallen, ensuring they will be taken care of for their sacrifice." He kissed my forehead. "It is us, all of us, who owe you for your sacrifice."

"It wasn't much of a sacrifice, given I'm still alive," I countered.

Solas tilted my head to the side and looked me in the eyes. "You gave your life, Perdi. It doesn't matter if you came back or not. You gave yourself willingly, knowing it meant death. You didn't go in thinking you'd come back. That, little Crow, is what true sacrifice is."

"When I was in the Gate, I called on Zephyr. He gave me back my pearl. But I thought he couldn't?" I asked.

"You saw only the link between you both, a vision of him when he touched the part of your soul he had. Your pearl has always kept you both connected," he answered and snarled for a heartbeat. His jealousy was thick in the air, but he swallowed it. "He couldn't give it back, not when you first asked for it. When I had asked him before why he wouldn't give it back, he said he was keeping it until you needed it. When you walked into the Gate, Zephyr stayed close by. He said you'd need him. He knew the Gate would kill you. He knew if you held on, if you wanted to come back, you'd need it." Solas kissed my bruised back. I was marked head to toe. "For a moment there, I didn't think you'd choose to live."

"For a moment, I almost didn't," I answered honestly. "But I couldn't give in. I had to try. I couldn't leave you all. And as much as I know this world brings suffering, it also brings love."

Zephyr had kept my secret, our secret. I was a Soul-Eater, and that reason alone was why I was alive, why I was given life again. I was surprised that Solas hadn't known. But Zephyr kept this even from his lifelong friend, Solas. He kept all of who he was from the one person he trusted most. If Zephyr didn't trust his king with this information, I would keep it for now. Some things were never meant to be said out loud, and some things weren't worth dying over.

"I thought..." Solas breathed me in, shuddering against me.

I rolled to face him. "It's okay, Solas. I'm here. You're not alone."

"I thought I'd lost you, and it was the most pain I have ever felt in my life. Nothing I have endured will ever compare to that moment. Up until then, I thought I was willing to pay anything to close that Gate, until I had to give you to it. It wasn't worth it. When I realized the cost would be you, I would have fought war after war instead of losing you." His voice shook. "And when we came home, and I saw the book and the letter, it broke my soul to know you knew you'd die, and you went to your death without me at your side. You went to your end alone, and it hurt all over again."

"It would have been worth it, even if I didn't make it, Solas. Because now I am the last Crow. For that, it would have been worth it."

"*My* Crow," he moaned into my mouth. He tasted like home. "But I will never risk you again, no matter what it costs me. I can't. Even if you hate me for it, I'd rather you alive hating me than the world losing its last Crow."

I didn't mind the word, hearing him utter it with love. I was the last, and I was his, as he was mine. I was both visions come true. Elda had seen me dead and stuck in Elphame. The reason she couldn't see which one would come to fruition was that both fates were mine to live. I died to close the Gate and came back to live in Elphame forever.

"I saw Aoife at the Gate." I breathed the words and smiled.

"I know," he replied. "She told me she saw you when she crossed into Elphame. Without you going into the fog, she wouldn't have trusted me, and none of this would have been possible."

"Fear nothing." I smiled and remembered the first time we met. "I've never feared you. I've wanted to, but I've always loved you. I knew you were as trapped as I was, but I kept the mask on like you told me. And every day that I tried to hate you, I only hated that you were stuck there like I was. When I would get angry, it wasn't because I hated seeing you. It was because I hated that you were there, stuck with me."

"I know. Whenever your fear flared, I saw you look for me. And once you saw me, your fear would vanish. You were both relieved to see me and sad to still see me. But that day you told me that you'd save me, I believed you and couldn't leave you to live in hell alone." His hot sigh rolled down my body. "And you did. You saved us all. You saved me, my people, our people, and the mortal realm. I knew you would."

Solas kissed my neck and shoulders, his fingers dancing ever so slightly down my side. The tickle sent my hips into his and his readiness. He nipped and licked my neck as I squirmed against him. He held me with his arm around my shoulders and pulled me tight to his body.

"I love you," he whispered.

"I finally made it home," I whispered into the night.

"*We* finally found our home."

* * * *

The prison was nothing like I thought it would be and nothing like it should have been for the likes of Faolan. For one, it smelled like my bedroom and was spotless. He had a view, a bed not bloodied from the last person and a bathroom that wasn't a bucket in the corner. If anything, he was on a forced vacation.

"The Dark Courts have no dungeons, little Crow. It was this or death," Solas whispered as we stepped into the room.

"I knew you'd close the Gate," Faolan said nonchalantly, like he wasn't shackled to a table and hadn't tasted freedom in weeks.

"You're looking well, Faolan," I said, just as casually. "Regrettably."

"You look like you've climbed up in life, from a simple Crow to what now? A lady of the Dark Court? How was that earned, Perdi? Did you enjoy currying favor in the Dark Courts? Was it worth it? Was what will come for us all worth the price you paid? I hope so, because you've only just begun paying for it."

I nodded. "A lady doesn't kiss and tell, but yes, it was every bit as enjoyable as I thought it would be. Thank you for asking."

Faolan leaned forward. "Ask yourself this… Are you willing to pay for what you've done, who you've tied yourself to? Because I very much doubt the rest of us are willing to cover the cost of you bedding the very blight of Elphame. Nothing here is free—not for me, not for him and now, not for you."

Solas stepped from the door with a growl, and I lifted my hand to stop him. "Those cornered will always bite. It is in our nature."

"We have so much in common now, Perdi. Both of us have suffered for that Gate." Faolan glared.

I laughed at the comment and motioned around his room. "Faolan, your idea of suffering and mine are two very different things. You don't know real suffering, and honestly, I hope you never experience what I have. But the day is young, and you seem to have a shovel and are digging yourself deeper and deeper every time you open your mouth."

"Suffering? You have no idea what real misery is until you've spent decades in these lands and been given impossible choices," Faolan scoffed, and for a moment, the disguise came down, and I saw a hint of who I'd once known.

"I was given an impossible choice. But I still made the right one."

"For you, for your people, for those you care about, for those who were weaker… You made an impossible choice to save them and not yourself, yes?"

I nodded.

"So did I, Perdi. I tried to save us all, but you couldn't see beyond your hate to the truth of what you would unleash." He shook his head as if clearing out memories. "You will learn that when you're at the top, that's where you truly suffer, and it never ends. There is no place anywhere in Elphame for peace. Every day you are forced to do things you never thought you'd do. To survive, to keep people you care about alive, you do what you must, regardless of the cost. You should know that as well as any other in this room. The very fact that you're still alive tells me you know all too well what must be done to keep above ground in Elphame. It is but a drop in the bucket of suffering yet to come."

I sat with his truth for a moment. "If you had told me the truth, I would have helped you, Faolan. And if I couldn't, I wouldn't hate you right now."

"The hardest part is that I know you would have tried," he answered. "But you would have died, so would I have—and so would my people."

"Would you do it again?" I asked. "Knowing you'd end up here?"

"Would you?"

"Yes," I answered without pause, because I would.

"As would I. I wish it hadn't been you. But I'd do it again even knowing now that it would be you to suffer. To keep what's coming from climbing out of her hellhole, I'd have done worse to better," he answered. It was probably the most honesty I had gotten from him since day one. "Why are you here? Have you come to finally kill me?"

I shook my head. "No, Faolan. There's been enough death, wouldn't you agree?"

He didn't answer. He rebuilt the mask he wore as a king, showing no fear, and stared with sorrow and rage in his eyes.

"I came because I need to let go, Faolan. I forgive the choices you were forced to make. I do know what it's like to be stuck between decisions, and each more impossible than the last, to make. I know that the very wind of Elphame pushes us into corners we can't get out of unless we do some godawful things—and I did. So, when I say I understand, I truly do. At one time, I didn't, and thought I could never hurt someone like you had hurt me. But I've been that desperate. I've been that scared, and I've done things I never thought I could have."

"Should I say thank you?" He smirked. "Is that what you're waiting for? Because we'll be here an awfully long time. There will never be a day I'm thankful for what you've done, and I fear, sooner or later, we'll be in the same position—filled with regret, both for different reasons."

"No, I don't need or want your thanks." I stood and pulled my leather gloves back on. "You're free from this prison, but you're not free from the suffering I've had to endure. You can live with it, just as I will. Enjoy that court and crown for the last minutes you have them."

His lips curled from anger into a smirk. "Little Crow—"

"This little Crow just gave you the life I wanted to take from you." Solas stopped Faolan from finishing his sentence and held out his hand to me.

I motioned to Zephyr to open the cell door. Elswyth stepped into the room, and I walked away. I got to the door and turned with a smile. "As I once said, my desire to see you fall, see your court fail, drastically outweighed everything you could possibly send my way. You sent me to hell, and I came back with your demons. Goodbye, Faolan."

"You said you forgave me!" he screamed.

"I do, but I've not forgotten, and I'm not the one holding the knife, am I?" I said and closed the door.

Solas leaned against the wall and grinned. "You would make the demons and devils of all the hells envious."

"Take me home, Solas." I grabbed his hand and held it tightly.

When I first stepped onto Elphame soil, I never imagined I'd be free. I yearned for it and for death, but never thought I'd taste true freedom or feel the breeze that carried the scent of home. From the moment I knew I loved Solas, I never allowed myself the possibility that I'd live, that I'd survive the closing of the Gate. Whenever I started to dream of a life with him, I'd stop myself. But here I was, here we were…together. Entire lives, mine and his, brought us freedom and a home we'd protect with our very lives. The suffering, the bleakness, the terror—it brought us to each other. There is no better way to end a life than by starting one new.

When the nightmares became too much, he ate the pain and fire within me. And when the darkness came, it was all mine. I lived within the night that ate this world, and I was exactly where I wanted to be. Home, with the monsters.

Elphame had taken the wrong Crow.

I was the last they'd Take.

I died for that title.

And I'd kill to keep it.

Chapter Thirteen

"Who is 'She'?" I asked, tucked into the safety of shadows, away from the eyes and ears of the Dark Courts.

I rolled my memories around in my head. I played them back and forth for myself and the shadows. I smelled and tasted each tear that had fallen when I'd died for Elphame. The Gate unwillingly gave me power the first time I'd come through. The second time, as it so desperately tried and failed to kill me, I'd used that stolen power to close it. I left the mist and the Gate's failure with answers. But with those answers came more questions and a web of treachery and trickery I couldn't unravel on my own.

You will try, and you will fail.

She will not allow this.

"Who is She? And what does She have to do with the Gates?" I asked again, unsure if I wanted to know or if I could allow myself the sweet mercy of ignorance.

"She is Blood and Bones," my shadows replied. "She sang the song that opened the Gate. The three Darkmore witches heard her call and helped create the path between worlds. She is the reason for this all and is the one who picks the Crows for kings."

"She should never have picked me," I answered.

"She did not—and did not want you here," they replied. "She didn't think you'd succeed at the Gate. And now, She is angry there are no more Crows. She will kill you if She can't use you."

"Elphame would be a better place without her."

My shadows shuddered against me. "Yes, before She finds a way to reopen the Gate."

"How do I stop her?" I asked.

"The same way She will try to stop you."

"Kill her," I answered.

"Kill her," they echoed. "She will find a way to use you and will use him to get to you."

I pondered for a moment, who *he* was, but already knew. Solas.

"She needs to die," I finally said. The swirl of my shadows told me they agreed.

"We hope you saved your mask. You'll need it again."

"I never took it off," I replied.

Want to see more from this author? Here's a taster for you to enjoy!

A Cursed Crow: The Song of Blood and Bones

Lanne Garrett

Coming August 2023

Excerpt

I was born twice, once of hope and once of horror—once of the mortal world and once of Elphame. The second time, the pain was mine alone to bear, and I came out twisted and broken, like the other creatures haunting these lands. Like everything else worth having in Elphame, survival wasn't mine to keep. I had merely chosen to die on a different day. Each day between now and then, when the end finally came with my name, would be a struggle for the next. The day I put on these wings was the last day I didn't hurt. I'd known it wouldn't be easy, but I'd been foolish enough to think it wouldn't be this bloody hard. That was my fate, as it was for each Crow before me—to be Taken from my home and brought into this land to suffer, to crave a home that I was not sure even existed anymore, one where my heart was whole, my body loved and my soul left untarnished and unbroken.

I had been told to accept who I was, who I had become—a Crow, a Wildling, a Soul-Eater, told to face the horror of it all or I'd never heal from it. But I wasn't born in the pits of hell like the rest of this new world. I was dragged through it, and it was all too much to carry on a broken back and with a soggy soul. I couldn't put my pieces back together when I didn't understand how I had gotten so broken and why I had been fated with this life. It was in our nature—mortals—to question every intricacy of life, to wonder, to grieve over the baggage we carried. And the person I had grown to count on, Solas, had no answers for me. He hid more within his dark soul than I dared to understand. He was the only one yet to remove the mask he'd carefully constructed in the Golden Court. He still wore his every day, and I wondered if he had ever spent a day without it. Even in all of his secrets and lies, I envied his ability to choose his next step with such ease and not crumble under the weight of each decision. But I suppose one did not become a king or maintain that throne with an iron fist by worrying over the small stuff, like the condition of his soul or anyone else's.

Like a game of chess, I played back every move that brought me into my living nightmare. From the moment I had met Nix, then Faolan, to me now sitting in the forest on the edge of Solas' territory in the Dark Court, I relived each memory in hopes I had missed a clue to my freedom. Solas had said I was free—but I wasn't, not really. I wasn't free from Elphame, free to go back to Whitwick. No matter what he said or what I tried to convince myself of, I was no freer with Solas than I had been before him. I merely sat in a different cage with enough windows to almost believe I was still wild. Deep inside, beyond the prison with no bars, my

Malice, my magick, threw itself against my ribs like a feral, caged animal. She craved release, but I couldn't risk it. I knew, with one misstep, the windows on my cage would be shuttered. I could see it in Solas' eyes when I would allow myself the courage to look. He, like me, sat on the edge of one wrong move, one bad decision, one shove over the edge. I had walked through hell, but my soul knew I was still there, and nothing I could do could change it.

Zephyr's shadows slinked around my ankles and darted between the grass and the woods. They slid along the earth as if no one owned them. It didn't matter how far they ventured. I could hear them in the back of my mind, like a soft melody playing in the background from miles away. We whispered our secrets and dissected our memories, always coming full circle to death. Everything in Elphame was solved in death. Countless lives were exploited until they couldn't beat their own hearts. For everything beautiful, there were hundreds of horrors. Every smile hid an ocean of tears. Every laugh had covered screams by the dozens. This place, Elphame, was a beautiful forest in the middle of hell. And the Dark Courts were just a roomier prison than my last. And like my previous one, I'd wreak havoc until I was let out.

I inched through the trees and motioned to the shadows, to the small wood and moss-built hut tucked into the thick underbrush, not twenty feet in front of me. "Ready?"

"We are, but are *you*?" the shadows replied.

I pulled my dagger from my pants and nodded. "He is the last in the Dark Courts to answer for what they did in Whitwick."

"Solas has asked you to stop hunting his people, that he would deal with it. He will not be happy."

"Does it look like I care what he has to say? He said he'd deal with it but hasn't. So, I will—and will do it in whatever manner I see fit," I answered. "They came to my home and killed my people."

"Garon did not *kill* your people."

"Yes, he did. He pushed a child in front of a horse to be trampled on the day of my Taking. He may not have wrung the child's life from his body, but he killed the boy, just the same." I groaned and paused against the tree. "Listen... If you don't want to help me, go home."

"We said we would, so we will. We just do not understand your need for vengeance. It consumes your humanity, which is the only thing that keeps you separate from the rest of Elphame."

"You don't get it. None of you do. Fae hunted us, and someone has to pay for it. It can't always be me who pays for what Fae did. Nix and I have spent weeks hunting them all down. If I have to suffer in Elphame, they can damn well suffer, too." I steadied myself once again. "Those who had no choice but to come, I left them with a pulse. I understand what it's like to be forced or have no choice. But those who came for no other reason than to revel in the death of children don't get to walk away without paying for it. Nothing is free, and this is their payment."

"We are glad this is the last. It is uncomfortable to watch," the shadows finally replied.

They didn't understand my need to punish those who tormented my people, who freely killed without penalty. We would always be lowly mortals if no one showed them any different. And I didn't care what Solas said. His people did not get to kill children and not suffer for it.

"Go grab him." I pointed my knife toward Garon's house. Garon was no bigger than I was and much less powerful. I had stalked him for days for this very moment. He knew I was there, and I knew he was terrified, just like the others had been. None of them liked the tables being turned, of finding themselves on the receiving end, hunted like animals.

With a blast of shadow, they were gone and ate up the ground like splashed ink, between Garon's hut and where I stood, waiting. I knew Solas wouldn't be pleased. But I didn't care, not as much as I should have. Zephyr wouldn't say a single thing about it because he knew it would be pointless to argue with me. When I first started hunting my enemies, Zephyr warned me that it wouldn't help extinguish the fire that burned in my soul, but he understood my need to snuff out what haunted my dreams. His understanding was the only reason the shadows had been allowed to help me. If Zephyr had disagreed, he'd have called them home, and I'd be out here alone. But I'd still be out here, and I'd still do what I needed to do. The shadows saved time, not lives.

Garon was spat onto the ground, half-dressed. He was a troll of a man, younger than most other trolls I had seen. His skin held a tint of green, like his hair, and not a single scar marred his body like they did mine. He jumped to his feet and spun in a circle, his green eyes widening when they landed on me. He took one step back, but the shadows were a black wall that gave him no space. He darted his eyes around as the wheels in his mind probably looked for a way out.

"Hello, Garon." I smiled. "I wouldn't run if I were you. You won't like what will happen if you force me to chase you down."

"Perdita," he replied. His voice was softer than I thought it would be. In my dreams, he had sounded monstrous, deep, rumbling. "What is the meaning of this?"

"I appreciate a man who gets straight to the point. I remember you, the day of my Taking," I answered, and his eyes grew wider. "The Dark Courts were forbidden to cross into Whitwick. They are not allowed to partake in the Taking of a Crow. Why, oh why, were you in the mortal realm, wreaking havoc?"

"Many of us went."

I nodded. "This is true, but those who went were forced. You went because you wanted to go."

"To refuse the call is to forfeit your life."

I rolled his words over in my mind. "I'll tell you what, Garon. I'll give you the same chance I gave everyone else I hunted down. You answer my questions, and I won't make you suffer."

He lifted his hands as if I would care he was unarmed. "I request a trial. You cannot kill me simply because I crossed the Gate. That decision is for the throne to make, not you."

"I'm not going to kill you for breaking Dark Court law," I answered. "But I'm going to make you suffer for taking the lives of my people. Whether you broke your laws to do it or not has nothing to do with me."

"I am Fae. My laws protect me. I request a trial."

"Alas, I am mortal, and my laws don't give a shit about you." I cleared the space between us and held my blade over his stomach. "You can choose your fate, unlike the choice given to me or my people. Answer my questions or suffer. Trust me when I tell you, your suffering will help me sleep better tonight."

He met my eyes and saw the truth. "What questions do you have of me?"

"You said that to refuse the call is to forfeit your life. Who made you go and why?"

He shook his head. "We're not allowed to talk about *Her*."

"She is blood and bones," I whispered, and he nodded. "Very well, if you can't talk about Her, I guess I've no more questions for you."

"Wait, wait…" His voice raised in panic. "I have other information you may like."

"Such as?"

"You must give me your oath that you won't kill me," he replied.

"I give you my oath. I won't kill you," I replied.

"You coming here wasn't a mistake."

"This isn't news to me, little troll."

"It should be. Haven't you ever wondered why only Wildlings have been called into Elphame? For decades, only Wilds have become Crows." His question piqued my curiosity. "The Caller of Crows has been looking for another Soul-Eater. With only one Soul-Eater in Elphame who is unbendable to her will, She calls on Wildlings in hopes of finding another."

"Why?"

He shrugged. "I don't know. Whenever we went to Whitwick, we were never allowed to harm a Wildling. We were told if we felt another Soul-Eater in Whitwick, we were to steal them back into Elphame, no matter the cost."

"And bring them to Her?" I asked, and he nodded. "Have you ever felt one there?"

"There is only one left, and he is already here. We've never felt another like him outside of Elphame," he answered. "Of all the Crows to come, you are who She hates the most."

I smiled. My secret was still safe. "Why does She hate me?"

His eyes grew wide as if I should have already known. "Because, Perdita, Solas stood against Her for you. You closed the Gate, and he let you live."

"Why should he kill me for that?"

He swallowed hard. "Wouldn't you wish to kill that which controls Solas?"

"I'm currently in that same boat, controlled by another," I replied. "That was worth your life, Garon."

My Malice flowed from me in a hot jerk and coated his body with my hate. I ate his energy in massive pulls and rolled his mind in my hands like a pearl. I pulled every drop of his magick from his soul and fought not to let him fall to the ground, a shriveled husk.

"But you gave me your oath." He groaned.

"I said I wouldn't take your life. I won't be the one to kill you. You've earned your life if you can make it back from the Sluagh. But remember this day, little troll, because it was the day I gave you a chance when you gave my people none. The next time I come, it will be for your life, and I won't give you the break I'm giving you now."

I motioned for the shadows, who picked his limp body up off the ground. They'd dump him in the caves of the Sluagh. If he made it out of there in one piece, without his magick, he'd have earned another day in a land that made us work for each and every one of them. And if he died, I'd feel nothing for his passing. He got the same chance I had been given when I came here—make it or die trying.

At that moment, I should have felt something more than satisfaction. It should have bothered me to punish the troll, but it didn't. It felt like crossing the last thing off a list. Like the others, Garon had come for my people and didn't expect me to come knocking. But now they'd know nothing was free, no matter what side of the Gate you stood on. I didn't kill any of them, but they certainly thought they'd die at my hands, just as my people thought they'd die at theirs. In my mind, we were almost even. *Almost.*

Garon, and those before him, were what it took for me to feel I wouldn't be hunted by the fog in my dreams. Those I could hunt down, I did, and I felt the balance restored as I exacted my revenge. I walked away and carried on as if I hadn't just terrorized a man, and it reminded me of how Solas and Zephyr could hold a conversation while in the middle of battle. To be honest, Garon, dead or alive, wasn't worth the mourning or guilt. The day he killed a child was the day he'd forfeited his own. So, I strolled through the forest and left whatever would become of him behind me, where it belonged. When the shadows returned, we didn't speak another word of what I had done. It was over. And I felt a little less broken because of it.

"Do you know why She is looking for another Finis?" I asked the shadows.

"Perhaps, if She were to get one at a young age, She could groom them into a shadow of herself. But outside of controlling Elphame with one, there is no other reason to risk trying to control a Soul-Eater," they replied. "She would be a fool to even try. Your kind is not easily controlled."

"Curious how Solas ended up with two of us," I answered and left it in the back of my mind to pick at later.

"He's not foolish enough to believe he could control either you or Zephyr."

"Yet, he tries."

"He'll die before that happens," they replied.

I rolled a shadow over my knuckles and released it back into its murky brethren, only to replace it with a new one. I practiced daily how to use my Finis' abilities without leaving a trail of soulless bodies behind me. Calling a soul without eating it or wanting to eat it would take decades to learn, if ever. The desire to keep pulling would never go away, or so Zephyr, the only other Soul-Eater alive, had informed me. With Garon, I felt that hunger to keep going. For now, I'd use souls already trapped, shadows, practice or I'd risk eating half of Elphame. Eating this world was much more appealing than leaving it whole. If all were gone, nothing but a whisper left in the shadows, I'd finally have peace. The want to end it all edged on a demand from my soul. What a sweet ending that would be.

Nix's voice drew me out of my twisted thoughts—a dark place my mind always went to when I was alone and there was no one to keep it at bay. I spent my days wandering, looking for a way back home, and when I couldn't find it, I looked for anything untainted to take my thoughts away from where I was. But the darkness was always there and always willing to hold my mind with ease. It was a sad life when the only peace was found in the dark, when the only ending in sight carried with it the destruction of all.

"I see you've paid a visit to Garon," Nix piped up from my side. "You smell like troll turd."

"Indeed. It was short and sweet. Unlike the others, I didn't have to chase the troll across half of Elphame. He was dumped in Sluagh territory, and I think he'll fare a little better than the last one I dumped there," I answered.

"My money is on the Sluagh."

I shouldn't have laughed, but I did. A broken heart made some things funnier than they should be. "He had a few interesting things to say, but nothing different than what the others already said."

"I've asked around, but no one knows why another Soul-Eater is needed. Some are speculating that it is to repopulate the Finis line."

I cringed. "Zephyr is family. That's just—"

"Gross," Nix finished my sentence. "No one wants to talk about it, given that mentioning Zephyr's name terrifies everyone. Your guess is as good as mine as to the why of it. Maybe it's for power or control—of what or why, I don't know. But no one in Elphame gets out of bed for less than that."

"I don't blame others for not wanting to talk about Zephyr. I wouldn't want to," I replied. "Did you hear anything else? Any news on the horn I've heard? That blasted thing hasn't shut up in weeks."

Just weeks after I had closed the Gate, the world popped like a bubble in my mind, and I woke to the blaring sound of a horn. Everything had slowed, and the wind screeched in my ears, but only for a moment. It was a long enough stretch of time for me to feel the edge of warning on the whine still hanging in the air. Of what I was being warned, I was yet to know. Sounds became sharp as a knife, yet dull and lifeless, as if the sound ate the energy around it and spit out something made of broken glass. Birds and insects fell silent, leaving only the sound of a horn in the distance. The world shimmered in my view, like looking out from inside the Gate. Since then, everything felt not quite right, off in some way, tilted slightly, just enough for me to notice. Each breath was like eating soupy air, thick and full, and burned my throat. The alarm had clawed at the back of my brain until I had told Nix. And still, the unease wouldn't leave entirely. It stained the air like rotting fruit. Every sound, every word, echoed with a whisper of a horn.

"I've heard nothing," he answered. "People always forget to look down, so I hear things not meant for my ears, but no one has mentioned it. Wouldn't it be easier for you to find out?"

"Since the war, no one speaks openly with me anymore, if at all. I don't think it would matter. It doesn't look like anyone else is hearing it. No one else responds to it." I rubbed the center of my chest. I released a long breath, trying to will the dread to leave. "It feels like fate is following me around, deciding when to brain me with a rock. Something is coming, and we better find it before it finds us."

"I've poked around, listened in, but there's no mention of any horn or a feeling of unease aside from the usual anxiety all of us feel in Elphame."

"Keep your ears open. Others may be holding their cards close to their chest, scared of what may happen if they were to show them."

"This is why I left this place, willingly. The games we play are tiresome. More of us would live if we weren't so ready to die in secret."

"It wouldn't be Elphame if we worked together," I replied dryly. But I couldn't blame anyone for wanting to save themselves over others. I had been there before, choosing between my life and that of others—and had chosen myself.

We walked through my favorite part of the forest, a place where small white flowers bloomed. They reminded me of snowdrops back home that burst through the frost to become the first beauty of the spring season. They reminded me that it didn't matter how harsh the conditions were. Beauty could still be found if I looked hard enough for it. Some days, I really had to dig for it. On other days, I stomped them out and cursed their beauty.

"Do you trust me, Perdi?" Nix asked.

"Of course." I smiled and felt that truth all the way to my soul. "I trust no one more than you."

"I feel the same." He looked up with a hearty smile. He was not my blood, but he was the only family I had brought from Whitwick Gates, my home. "Perdi, I need you to come with me and ask no questions. Today, I need your trust more than ever."

"Whenever anyone asks for blind trust, it's either going to hurt or it's going to make me mad. Which one will it be?"

"Both. Yeah, probably both." His smile vanished.

Both it would be.

I frowned for a moment but followed him anyway. I was curious, not fearful. Of all the things that Nix was, the reason for my death would not be one of them.

About the Author

Lanne Garrett writes books. Considering where you're reading this, it makes perfect sense. She lives in Vancouver, here she spends her days getting lost in the beauty of reading and writing and can be found behind a mountain of books on any given Sunday.

Lanne loves to hear from readers. You can find her contact information, website details and author profile page at https://www.finch-books.com

FINCH
BOOKS

www.ingramcontent.com/pod-product-compliance
Lightning Source LLC
LaVergne TN
LVHW041925090826
845145LV00015B/696

* 9 7 8 1 8 0 2 5 0 5 4 2 9 *